"It's the Kobayashi Maru *all over again!" Roger yelled.*

Jean-Luc Picard felt a moment of doubt. Every Academy cadet knew of the legendary *Kobayashi Maru* scenario, a training exercise in which nothing a cadet did could succeed. Could it be? Possibly. But if it wasn't—

"We have only ten minutes left," Jean-Luc said.

"Do something, Jean-Luc," Marta said. "Give the word, and I'll change course—"

"Shut up!" Roger shouted. "That's mutiny!"

Jean-Luc looked at him. Roger was sweating, his eyes darting frantically. Marta was right: For Jean-Luc or even the upperclassman Tom Franklin, to assume command, they all would have to mutiny against Roger's authority, breaking one of the oldest laws of the service. If this were just a test, that was a step that could well mean the end of their Starfleet dreams. . . .

Available from MINSTREL Books

STAR TREK

THE NEXT GENERATION®

STARFLEET ACADEMY™ #9

NOVA COMMAND

Brad and
Barbara Strickland

Interior illustrations by
Todd Cameron Hamilton

A MINSTREL®
BOOK

Published by POCKET BOOKS
New York   London   Toronto   Sydney   Tokyo   Singapore

This book is a work of fiction. Names, characters, places and incidents are products of the author's imagination or are used fictitiously. Any resemblance to actual events or locales or persons, living or dead, is entirely coincidental.

A MINSTREL PAPERBACK *Original*

A Minstrel Book published by
POCKET BOOKS, a division of Simon & Schuster Inc.
1230 Avenue of the Americas, New York, NY 10020

STAR TREK is a Registered Trademark of
Paramount Pictures.

A VIACOM COMPANY

This book is published by Pocket Books, a division of Simon & Schuster Inc., under exclusive license from Paramount Pictures.

ISBN: 0-671-51009-6

First Minstrel Books printing December 1995

10 9 8 7 6 5 4 3 2 1

A MINSTREL BOOK and colophon are registered trademarks of Simon & Schuster Inc.

Cover art by Catherine Huerta

Printed in the U.S.A.

For three wonderful teachers:
Mr. Shirley, Mrs. Gilbert, and Mr. Bray

STARFLEET TIMELINE

2264

The launch of Captain James T. Kirk's five-year mission, _U.S.S. Enterprise,_ NCC-1701.

2292

Alliance between the Klingon Empire and the Romulan Star Empire collapses.

2293

Colonel Worf, grandfather of Worf Rozhenko, defends Captain Kirk and Doctor McCoy at their trial for the murder of Klingon chancellor Gorkon.

Khitomer Peace Conference, Klingon Empire/Federation (_Star Trek VI_).

2323

Jean-Luc Picard enters Starfleet Academy's standard four-year program.

2328

The Cardassian Empire annexes the Bajoran homeworld.

2341

Data enters Starfleet Academy.

2342

Beverly Crusher (née Howard) enters Starfleet Academy Medical School, an eight-year program.

2346

Romulan massacre of Klingon outpost on Khitomer.

2351

In orbit around Bajor, the Cardassians construct a space station that they will later abandon.

2353

William T. Riker and Geordi La Forge enter Starfleet Academy.

2354

Deanna Troi enters Starfleet Academy.

2356

Tasha Yar enters Starfleet Academy.

2357

Worf Rozhenko enters Starfleet Academy.

2363

Captain Jean-Luc Picard assumes command of U.S.S. Enterprise, NCC-1701-D.

2367

Wesley Crusher enters Starfleet Academy.

An uneasy truce is signed between the Cardassians and the Federation.

Borg attack at Wolf 359; First Officer Lieutenant Commander Benjamin Sisko and his son, Jake, are among the survivors.

U.S.S. Enterprise-D defeats the Borg vessel in orbit around Earth.

2369

Commander Benjamin Sisko assumes command of Deep Space Nine in orbit over Bajor.

Source: Star Trek® Chronology / Michael Okuda and Denise Okuda

NOVA COMMAND

CHAPTER

1

Jean-Luc Picard was not used to marching in formation. Back on the vineyard his family called home, he was almost always running rather than marching, either alone or with his older brother, Robert. But here at Starfleet Academy, he was rapidly getting used to doing things Starfleet's way, not his way. He squirmed a little inside his stiff new uniform, the September sun hot on his face and neck. Or maybe that was just the heat of self-consciousness—

"Cadets, attention! Right turn! Forward, march, at the double!"

Jean-Luc swallowed, made the movements as sharply as he could, and hoped no one noticed how nervous he was on his first day as a Starfleet cadet. He tried to keep in step as his file, like eleven others, marched into a great white building marked Scobee Hall. He blinked as he passed through the open doorway, going from sunlight to soft artificial gloom. The tramp of marching feet faded to a soft, rhythmic *clump-clump* on the red carpet.

Through another door, and Jean-Luc entered a vast auditorium, its air-conditioning cool in contrast to the hot day outside. Ahead of him the file turned smartly right, and he saw the cadets were moving to take a row of seats. *Don't let me have to start a new row,* he begged the powers that looked out for raw cadets. *I don't want to walk across in front of everyone!*

Maybe they heard. To his relief, Jean-Luc found himself almost in the middle of the row. Like the female cadet ahead of him, he halted, did a precise quarter-turn, and stood at attention before his seat. Through the rows of cadets ahead of him, he could barely see the stage. A group of men and women, all in Starfleet uniform, sat there, gazing out at the sea of new faces. No one spoke a word. The cool air of the auditorium smelled scrubbed and lifeless, not like the scent-laden breezes back on the vineyard, rich with the odors of grapes and soil and growing things. Minutes passed, and at last even the muffled footsteps fell silent.

Then onstage the man in the central chair stood and approached a lectern, tugging his admiral's tunic into position as he came forward. He had a craggy, seamed face and a brush of gray hair, and there was something a little unfamiliar about his features, a little alien. He tilted his head and swept his gaze around the auditorium. With a half smile, he said, "At ease, cadets. You may be seated."

Jean-Luc sank back into the chair behind him, and for the first time he looked around. The cadet who had been behind him sat at his left. He was taller than Jean-Luc, with close-cut blond hair, an aristocratic nose, and an arrogant tilt to his chin. To Jean-Luc's right was a pretty dark-haired girl, looking uncomfortable in her new uniform. She did not look at Jean-Luc, but sat biting her lip and staring at the man onstage. Jean-Luc realized she was just as scared as he was. He hoped he didn't show it quite as much.

The man onstage said, "Welcome, cadets. I am Admiral Silona, and I am the superintendent of Starfleet Academy. I know you have all come here to work hard and to succeed. I wish you well. However, right now I want each of you to look first to your left, then to your right."

Jean-Luc's face felt hot. He had jumped the gun already. But he turned to stare into the girl's worried eyes. Admiral Silona continued to speak: "Each of you has seen two other cadets. Counting yourself, you now know three hopeful young people. Well, one of you isn't going to make it through the next four years."

Fear flashed in the girl's dark eyes. Jean-Luc, who felt as if Admiral Silona were talking directly to him, forced himself to grin in a cocky, know-it-all way. "We'll see about that," he whispered. His neighbor gave him a weak smile in return.

Admiral Silona introduced other officials, officers in

1995

charge of class scheduling, housing, and other details. Then he paused for a moment before resuming: "No matter whether you are among the one-third who will drop out of the Academy or the two-thirds who will see it through to the end, we hope your time with us is a time of learning and growth. It has always been a tradition at Starfleet Academy to begin each new term with a convocation of first-year cadets like this. We traditionally have a speaker who will give you young people a few words of wisdom. I can honestly say that I have dozed through more than one of these speeches." The cadets laughed, all of them sounding uncertain and nervous.

The admiral smiled. "Well, I do not plan to sleep through today's address. Cadets, I will not give our speaker a long introduction, because he needs none. In his long career he has become so well known that each and every one of you will recognize his name. Therefore, rather than be flowery, I will merely ask you to join me in welcoming retired Starfleet Admiral Spock."

Jean-Luc gasped as the curtains parted and a tall, lean figure stepped forward. Admiral Spock wore a dark-blue robe rather than a uniform, and he moved slowly, but he had an air of great dignity about him. He nodded toward Admiral Silona in a Vulcan gesture of greeting, and Jean-Luc noted his keen, intelligent features.

The audience fell silent for a respectful moment. Then someone applauded, and everyone joined in. Clapping enthusiastically, Jean-Luc rose, and the cadets followed his lead, giving the speaker a standing ovation. Admiral Spock stood at the lectern, his head tilted, one eyebrow lifted in a look of quizzical patience. When at last the applause died down and the cadets had sat again, he began softly: "It is an honor to welcome a new generation of Starfleet officers."

Jean-Luc sat entranced as Spock spoke briefly and simply of the duties the cadets were taking upon themselves. Spock pointed out that the galaxy was a huge place, still barely explored, and that new discoveries, new life-forms, new civilizations awaited them all. He barely mentioned his own career as a Starfleet science officer and diplomat, though everyone in the auditorium knew his story quite well. Spock and the other members of the *U.S.S. Enterprise* had become part of Starfleet lore, and listening to him was like listening to a legend come to life. Spock ended by wishing them all a good experience at Starfleet Academy and by reminding them that the greatest exploration was the expansion of knowledge. Then, holding his right hand out, forming a *V* between his outspread index and middle finger on one side and ring finger and pinkie on the other, he said, "I leave you with a Vulcan expression of farewell. Live long and prosper."

The cadets applauded again, so long that Admiral Silona at last had to hold up his hands for silence. "Admiral Spock has time for a few questions," he said. "I am sure there must be one or two out there."

After an uncomfortable pause, the cadet on Jean-Luc's left stood. Admiral Silona nodded toward him and said, "Identify yourself, cadet, and ask your question."

"Cadet Roger Wells, sir," said the young man in an

6

enviably clear and confident voice. "We've all heard of the battles the *Enterprise* had with Romulans, Klingons, and other enemies. I would like to know, Admiral Spock, how it feels to be in combat."

Spock's expression did not change. He said, "Your question is illogical, Cadet Wells. I am a Vulcan. Our emotions—our feelings, as you put it—are under control at all times. Human emotions are on a different plane and of a different type. Therefore I can give you no clear idea of how you might feel in combat. However, let me say that my own mood at such times was always one of disappointment. Each time two sentient species fight, someone has failed. I urge you not to prefer combat to peaceful means of solving your problems."

When someone else asked a question, Roger Wells turned toward Jean-Luc with a smirk on his face. "I heard he was a hero, but I guess he's just become old and soft," he muttered. "Oh, well, another illusion shattered."

Jean-Luc glared at him. He was so angry that he did not trust himself to speak—at least not to Roger Wells. Instead he stood to signal that he had a question to ask, but others were ahead of him. At last Admiral Silona said, "We have time for one more question." He squinted into the auditorium. His gaze met Jean-Luc's and it was almost as if the admiral could read Jean-Luc's desperate thought: *Me! Pick me!* "You there in the center." Admiral Silona gestured toward him.

Jean-Luc cleared his throat. "Cadet Jean-Luc Picard. Admiral Spock, you have had experiences that we have

8

never known, yet at one time you were just like us, a new cadet with your whole career before you. If you were in our place, just beginning your studies, what advice would you most wish to hear?"

Spock looked at him for a long time. He made a tent of his fingers and gazed over it as he appeared to consider the question. At last he spoke. "I would say my best advice is this: See each crisis as an opportunity. Never believe you have learned all you need to know. And whenever possible, find a way to turn an adversary into an ally. If you can do these things, you will be a successful Starfleet officer."

The experience of having spoken to a Starfleet legend lifted Jean-Luc's heart. He hardly minded the march back out into the sunlight, the dispersal to academic stations, the business of getting his class schedule and registration information. In the mess hall he barely noticed what he ate—except to observe that the replicated food wasn't nearly as good as his mother's French cooking. And in the early afternoon the round of orientation sessions and lectures seemed to fly by.

It was only later, after the evening meal, that reaction set in. He realized then that he had not even asked the girl cadet her name—a pity, because she looked like someone who needed a friend as badly as he did. He reflected that he had no acquaintances at Starfleet Academy, that he knew no one here, halfway around the world from his home. And he began to worry again about the possibility of failure.

For Jean-Luc had faced a long and hard struggle in coming to Starfleet Academy. A year earlier he had failed the entrance examination. Then this year he had to resort to deception to try again, because his father, Maurice Picard, was dead set against his leaving the vineyard to try to make a career in space. The strains and stress that his decision had put on the family worried Jean-Luc, and he was sure his father would never feel the same toward him again. Now here he was, a year older than most of the other cadets, feeling as if he stood out like a Klingon at a Vulcan wedding.

It would have helped if Jean-Luc had even one friend to confide in, but he was a stranger here. His roommate, a quiet, dark young man named Jomo Nkolo, was polite but distant, as if he were always listening to some music played just too softly for Jean-Luc to hear. The closest they came to a real conversation was during dinner, when Jomo said, "You asked a very good question this morning, I thought."

Jean-Luc smiled. "I almost didn't get to ask it at all. I'm glad Admiral Silona could read my mind when I was hoping he would call on me."

Jomo nodded as he reached for the bread. "Yes, that is an advantage to being a Betazoid."

Once more Jean-Luc felt foolish. Of course—*Silona* was a Betazoid name, and Betazoids were all telepathic. Maybe the admiral really *had* picked up Jean-Luc's thoughts. If he were that good, Jean-Luc reflected, the cadets would really have to watch their step around the superintendent!

10

Then Jomo had to report to pick up his computer padd and datapacks, and when he got back he was so interested in the devices that he had no time for conversation. Jean-Luc had to report for physical assessment at the end of the day, and although he made a good showing on the treadmill and other tests, by the time he returned to their dorm room he was exhausted. That evening as he and Jomo prepared for lights out, they exchanged hardly a dozen words.

Their room was near the top of Newell Dormitory,

the temporary home of more than a thousand first-year cadets. Standing at the window, staring out into the dark, Jean-Luc could see the distant lights of San Francisco, the archaic but charming sweep of the old Golden Gate Bridge, now a monument. It was all strange and new, and he was a bit frightened. "Darken," he ordered the room computer, and the window obediently became opaque. In the darkness he lay back on his bed. Across the room Jomo was already snoring softly.

Jean-Luc crossed his arms behind his head and gazed into the empty darkness, thinking of Admiral Silona's assurance: One out of three cadets would never make it through the four-year program.

Jean-Luc clenched his teeth and smiled without much joy.

One out of three.

Well, he thought, *we'll see about that.*

CHAPTER

2

Whenever he looked back at his first month at Starfleet Academy, Jean-Luc Picard would always have the impression of doing thousands of things at once, of getting by on too little sleep, and of covering up his secret fear of failing with a show of nerve. And yet, it was all a blur: hustling from class to class, learning from lecturers or from computers, running on the track as if something were chasing him.

Being good at track was his one great consolation. He was an excellent runner, and within the first week of school the junior varsity track team invited him to join. That was an unusual privilege for a beginning cadet, and he accepted the invitation at once. It should have been a real honor. However, it wasn't enough. Having barely clawed his way into the Academy, Jean-Luc was determined to be the very best at everything.

Only he wasn't.

Others often proved just a little better than Jean-Luc. And far too often the other person proved to be Roger Wells. Their competition reached a peak during an important examination in Continuum Distortion Topology. Jean-Luc had studied for days, trying to master the fiendishly difficult mathematics of four-dimensional space. Continuum Distortion Topology was a kind of geometry of warped space and twisted time. The mathematics involved allowed a starship to maneuver safely while in warp drive, and computers always handled the work.

The problem was that Starfleet cadets had to understand exactly how the computers did that work, so they had to be able to do it, too.

Fifty other cadets sweated through the exam. They were in a large lecture room, each cadet at a separate desk, each one bent over a computer padd, each one struggling to juggle space, time, and relative speed in equations that sometimes went on for a hundred lines of figures and symbols. Talking was not allowed, so the cadets worked with old-fashioned keypads, tapping in the information, locking the data in memory, and asking the computer to perform the intricate steps of the formulas they created. Soft taps and clicks filled the air, punctuated occasionally by a quiet groan as some cadet realized he or she had left out a step or had reached the wrong answer.

Jean-Luc's fingers were slippery with sweat as he keyed in the final line of the last problem, a line thick with deltas, omegas, Vulcan sadors, and other mathematical symbols. With a final triumphant keystroke, Jean-Luc executed the program. A few moments later a chime sounded and a chorus of student moans broke out all around the room. Time was up, and the computer padds had locked them out. An instantaneous grading program began. The entire, devilishly hard exam would be scored in just a few seconds.

Leaning forward, Jean-Luc studied the screen built into his desk. Grading included points for both accuracy and speed. He was sure that this time he had solved every problem—

His groan joined the others. The class scores glowed on the screen before him. His student number, E-A1737, was in second place. One other student had beaten him, by no more than half a second. That student's number was E-L1004. Student numbers were private, but everyone knew that one.

It belonged to Roger Wells.

"Yes! A 4.0!" Roger crowed, staring at the screen. Then he turned to Jean-Luc. "Oh, Picard, congratulations on your 3.97. Not bad—for a *farmer*." His grin was wicked.

"Thank you, Roger," Jean-Luc returned in a dry voice. "It's true that not all of us have fathers in the diplomatic service who can afford to educate us privately. We simply scrape along the best we can."

Students were picking up their padds, some of them looking truly dejected. CDT mathematics was the first huge hurdle that many Academy students faced, and it was the reason that as many as a tenth of any first-year class washed out. Roger came over and gave Jean-Luc a hearty slap on the shoulder. "I like a man who knows how to take defeat. Then again, it may be genetic. You know, I'm descended from the Duke of Wellington who cooked your ancestors' goose at Waterloo."

Jean-Luc tucked his padd under his arm and walked toward the door, away from that insulting hand. "Yes, so you've said."

"Ah, well, as long as you're used to coming in second, it must not be so bad. Although it probably means you don't have a hope of being named to a Nova team."

Jean-Luc bit his lip to hold in his irritation. The fair-haired Roger might not be telepathic, but he certainly had an instinct for the right way to make a fellow angry. "We'll see about that." In his month at the Academy, that had become almost his motto.

"Face it," Roger said as he followed Jean-Luc out into the milky light of an overcast day. "No more than ten first-year cadets have ever been named to Nova teams. This term there are what, twelve of these CDT classes? I'd say your chances are pretty slim, friend."

"And I'd say it depends on the scores the other students make. A 4.0 is unusual, Roger. I dare say that even a 3.97 is respectably high. It could just be that the two best CDT students happen to be in the same class."

"I wouldn't bet on that," Roger said. "I'll see you later, Picard." He strode away, and for a moment Jean-Luc looked after him, envy in his heart.

Roger Wells *might* become an excellent starship captain in time. He *might* carve out a brilliant career. He *might* win the loyalty of his crew.

But somehow Jean-Luc didn't believe it would happen. Roger's father, an important diplomatic minister in the Federation government, had made things too easy for his son. Roger didn't have to struggle for anything. He never seemed to worry about grades or studying, and he certainly never seemed to spend days going over and over the same material the way Jean-Luc did. And now he obviously thought that he had a guaranteed spot on the Nova teams.

Jean-Luc sighed. Every first-year cadet longed for an appointment to a Nova trainer. The lucky few who were team members would get their first taste of duty in space. True, the little ships were not equipped with warp drive and were limited to the solar system, but serving aboard a Nova trainer gave cadets a far better sense of space duty than any simulation could. Then, too, the Nova cadets were on their own, operating the ship without any interference or help from Starfleet personnel, and so being on the teams was a badge of honor, a mark of confidence.

And, to tell the truth, it was also something to boast about. Not that Jean-Luc would ever boast—at least not as much as the conceited Roger—

Someone tugged at his arm. "I said hi three times!" a girl's voice complained. "You might at least answer me."

Jean-Luc turned and looked into the bright eyes of the girl who had sat next to him at the convocation.

17

"Hello," he said with a grin. "I've been looking for you for weeks."

She made a face at him. "Not very hard."

"No, honestly, I've been scanning the whole campus for you. I never learned your name."

With a look of mock exasperation she said, "And you didn't think to check for my picture in the database."

Jean-Luc slapped his forehead. "What a dolt I am! I never even thought of that. All I'd have to do would be to look at six thousand pictures, and one of them would be you."

She wrinkled her nose and stuck out her tongue. "First of all, you'd only have to look at human girls. That would mean only about two thousand pictures. Second, you could set your computer to search for my hair and eye color. That would bring it down to a few hundred. Still, I guess that's too much work for a boy, Jean-Luc Picard."

Jean-Luc blushed. "You actually went to all that trouble to find my name?"

She laughed. "Not exactly. You identified yourself when you asked your question, remember?"

He joined in her laughter. "I *am* a dolt. Well, let's introduce ourselves at once. I'm Jean-Luc Picard, of Labarre, France, first-year cadet and professional nervous wreck."

She grinned and held out her hand. "Marta. Marta Batanides, of Centauri colony Helene. Also first-year and not quite the wreck I was on that first day, thanks to you."

Jean-Luc glanced at the clock on the Student Center tower. "I have a break right now," he said. "How about you?"

"Nothing before Personal Combat. I've got thirty minutes."

"Let's get a snack."

The Student Center terrace overlooked the Pacific, a deep blue on this cloudy morning. A fresh, salty breeze came in from the ocean. Jean-Luc and Marta found a table and sat there to have a drink and munch their snacks. Jean-Luc gave Marta a quizzical glance. "You said you're not as nervous as you were, thanks to me. What did you mean?"

She shrugged. "Oh, it's just the way you reacted when Admiral Silona assured us that a third of the class won't make it. You seemed so confident that I guess a little of it rubbed off on me. Anyway, classes aren't as bad as I thought they might be. I'm doing better than I ever expected. Topped out in my CDT class, in fact."

"Did you?"

She grinned with pleasure. "Darn right I did. Scored 3.88, a whole decimal place ahead of the guy who came in second. I think I've got a real shot at a Nova appointment."

"Well, I hope you make it."

She sipped her raspberry soda and said, "So how did you do?"

"Came in second," he admitted.

Marta gave him a look of commiseration. "Oh, Jean-Luc, I'm sorry."

Jean-Luc glanced away, not willing to tell her that even coming in at second place in his class, he had beaten her score. "Well, that's the way it happens."

They talked for a few minutes more, Marta giving him a hilarious account of her trip to the solar system from Alpha Centauri. It was a short hop, not much more than four light-years, but the ship had been a slow commercial cruise vessel full of teenagers of seven or eight different species off on a tour of the local star systems. On the second day of the six-day voyage, when the food replicators began assuming that everyone liked the taste of the Klingon food, a revolt almost broke out. And when the sonic showers developed a malfunction that turned everyone's skin a bright shade of green, pandemonium reigned. "If I could survive that trip," Marta said at last, "then Starfleet Academy should be a snap. Uh-oh, time to run to class. Can we see each other tomorrow, Jean-Luc?"

Jean-Luc made a face. "I wish we could, but I've already signed up for the marathon team tryouts. How about this weekend?"

"Sorry," Marta said. "That's our four-day break, and I promised my mom and dad I'd fly to Luna Station Copernicus to visit my great-aunt Sara. I haven't seen her in ages, and I can't back out of this trip. We'll just leave it open, all right?"

"Fine," Jean Luc said. They parted company, and Jean-Luc walked toward the gymnasium. Exam period meant that the normal rush had eased off a bit. His physical-training class did not meet that day, but he always used any free time to get in a little running or to work off some steam in weight lifting, calisthenics, or swimming.

He went into the gym from the front and walked past some noisy games of basketball and indoor volleyball. He was heading for the locker rooms when he caught sight of a familiar blond figure. Roger Wells was just going into the fencing arena.

Jean-Luc's lips curved into a smile. He was good at many sports, but his best two were running—and fencing. In fact, Jean-Luc had captained the All-Europe youth fencing team while still a junior in high school. So Roger was a fencer, was he? Well, here was a chance to take him down a peg or two. If anyone could stand a little dose of humility, it was Roger Wells.

Jean-Luc went to the fencing equipment desk and checked out a sweatsuit, shoes, and mask. He regretted that he had not brought his own fencing foil, but he tested a dozen before finally deciding he liked one, a light, well-balanced rapier that felt perfect in his hand.

When he entered the arena, only one fencer was there. It had to be Roger, though the hood and mask covered his face. He was practicing alone, going through the intricate movements and exercises of the difficult Ellipsian attack and defense.

"Care for a pass or two?" Jean-Luc asked, approaching the masked figure.

Roger turned, shrugged, bowed, and stepped into the fencing circle. With a smile, Jean-Luc tugged his mask into place, adjusted his hood, and made a few practice moves. "It's been a long time since I did this," he said, trying to sound humble and sincere. "Please excuse me if I'm a little rusty."

They crossed swords, and then Roger launched his first attack, a simple set of movements aimed more at letting them both warm up than at providing any real threat. Jean-Luc easily parried, then riposted with a wicked forward lunge that nearly caught his opponent off-guard. They broke apart, and then with more respect than before, Roger tried an Ellipsian gambit, an intricate set of thrusts and parries worked out first on a low-gravity world and then adapted to Earth standards. Not many fencers could keep up an Ellipsian attack for more than a few minutes before dropping from exhaustion.

Jean-Luc had studied Ellipsian techniques, and his runner's stamina served him well. The problem with the Ellipsian approach to fencing was that under the heavy gravity of Earth, the movements quickly wore you out. He risked collapse, though, keeping up with Roger blow for blow and returning the thrusts with interest.

By the third pass, neither of the two had managed to score a single hit. Inside his mask, Jean-Luc was sweating. Salty drops ran into his eyes, blurring his vision. Ellipsian fencing was devilishly hard work, but if Roger could stand it, so could he. Neither gained an advantage that pass or the next, but then Jean-Luc's opponent seemed to find a new burst of energy, just when his own stamina was fading. He forced Jean-Luc back, and Jean-Luc danced away, playing for time, watching for an opening.

The killing thrust came from nowhere. Jean-Luc gasped as the blunted foil's button pressed against his chest, right on the heart-shaped target. He had not seen it coming and had no way to avoid it.

"Touché," said an unfamiliar voice. Jean-Luc's opponent reached up, swept off the mask, and pushed the hood back.

It was not Roger at all. It was a sandy-haired, healthy-looking older student, someone Jean-Luc had never seen before. "I yield," he gasped, utterly winded.

"Yield, nothing," the tan young man said with a grin. "Jean-Luc Picard, you are dead!"

CHAPTER

3

Jean-Luc's victorious opponent swept his hood off. His mop of brownish-blond hair, parted in the middle, was plastered down with sweat. He had a long, intelligent-looking face, ironic blue eyes, and an expression of respect as he held out his hand. "You're good, Mr. Picard. Ever thought of going out for the fencing team?"

Jean-Luc shook the stranger's hand. "I fenced in high school and didn't do too badly, but here at the Academy I think I'll stick to track. You are—?"

The older boy rested the tip of his foil on the floor and twirled the hilt. "My name's Tom Franklin. As of next week, I'll be the new captain of the varsity fencing team. Hope you'll change your mind—for your first term it would be just junior varsity, but with a little practice, you could be a real asset to the senior team."

"I don't know about that. I should have been able to keep up the pace, but you wore me down." Jean-Luc pulled his hood back, feeling the air cool on his sweaty face and neck. "I can hardly lift my foil. You're not even breathing hard. Are you from Ellipsias?"

With a grin, Franklin shook his head. "I've spent some time on Mars, which has even lower gravity than Ellipsias, but I wasn't born there. I'm from the southeastern section of North America, actually. My family's sort of a stew of German, Irish, English, and a long time ago, Cherokee."

"Somewhere back there you must have had one or two fencing ancestors," Jean-Luc said. He was finally beginning to get his breath again. The older boy had really pressed him, and even his runner's conditioning hadn't been much help.

Franklin led the way to the equipment window, where both he and Jean-Luc turned in their foils and masks. The older cadet said, "You're good. Don't sell yourself short. You just haven't had enough experience with exotic fencing techniques. I thought you might not be able to counter an Ellipsian attack, but I wasn't sure I could outlast you. It does call for a lot of energy."

"I suppose you practice Ellipsian techniques a great deal?" asked Jean-Luc.

With a shrug, Franklin said, "I keep in condition, yes. Actually, it isn't fencing that gave me enough steam to wear you down. I've been playing an interesting game from the pre-Columbian Native American era. It's a form of stickball, pretty intense and pretty exhausting. The name of the game is *toli*. Ever heard of it?"

Jean-Luc admitted he had not. "Hard to play?"

"Well, it can be. You need a reasonably level patch of ground, two posts to serve as goals, and an irregularly-shaped ball. Oh, and you also need a couple of teams made up of people who don't mind going a little bit crazy with effort and strain. The game plays hard and fast and long. Great way to stay in shape, though—that's what gave me the wind to carry through with the Ellipsian maneuvers. I've put together a team, and we occasionally travel to the tournaments the Native American Nations hold."

It sounded intriguing to Jean-Luc. He asked, "Is *toli* a Starfleet Academy-sanctioned game? I haven't seen it in the official athletic catalog."

"No, we play it in our free time," Franklin said.

Jean-Luc laughed. "What's that?"

Franklin's grin was understanding. "It's what you get if you survive first year. But, as I was saying, the game is all informal. Next time we schedule a practice, I'll give you a call. If you have the time, you can take a look and see if you want to learn the game." At the door to the showers, Franklin tilted his head quizzically. "By the way, why did you offer to fence with me?"

Jean-Luc sighed and shook his head. "To tell you the truth, I thought you were someone else. I saw Roger Wells come into the gym, and I mistook you for him."

"Oh, him." Franklin shrugged. "He's interested in the fencing team, and we've had an exchange or two."

"Is he going to be on the team?" asked Jean-Luc.

"I don't think so," Franklin replied. "Technically he's pretty good, but he doesn't have half your style. Just between the two of us, I'd much rather have you on the team than Roger Wells. Anyway, he just looked in to tell me he couldn't give me a match this afternoon. I was glad you showed up. That gave me a substitute first-year cadet to humiliate."

"So glad to have been of service," said Jean-Luc drily. "I enjoyed it. See you around."

The long holiday weekend approached with Jean-Luc in a discontented, brooding mood. Back in September when Jean-Luc had parted from his father, Maurice, the two had achieved a surface calm after a long season of stormy arguments. But Maurice's grudging good wishes barely hid the bitter disappointment that he had felt when his favorite son had chosen to enter Starfleet Academy rather than remain to work in Maurice's beloved vineyard. Jean-Luc's occasional calls home had ended more than once with Maurice insisting that his son would, in time, reconsider his decision, decide that tradition mattered more than adventuring in outer space, and come back to Labarre for good.

Now Jean-Luc knew that if he returned for the long weekend his father would try all his skill at persuading him to give up his ambition to explore the far reaches of the galaxy. Jean-Luc knew just how it would go: First Maurice would make clumsy jokes, then he would coax, then he would bluster, and finally it would all end in a furious argument. Jean-Luc would refuse to resign from the Academy, Maurice would explode, and the whole meeting would wind up with both of them angry and unreasonable. Jean-Luc had been there before.

In the end, he decided that he just was not ready to risk that kind of confrontation again. Instead of flying home, he settled into a private holophone booth and called his mother at a time when he knew his father would be working in the vineyard. She answered at once, looking a little disheveled—harvest time was always a busy time, and even Yvette Picard showed some signs of being rushed, even if only in a few strands of hair being out of place. Her eyes lit up at once when she saw who was calling. "Jean-Luc! How lovely to see you."

"Hello, Mother," he said. Now that her image was present before him, sitting at the desk in his father's office—the only room in the house where the fiercely old-fashioned Maurice permitted a computer terminal and holophone—Jean-Luc felt his heart give a little lurch. Just the sight of her, and the glimpse he caught of the room behind her, made him homesick.

"Why are you calling? Are you all right?" she asked, worry in her voice.

He smiled, trying to look reassuring and confident. "Perfectly. I'm keeping very busy here, but I think of you often. I miss you."

"You don't look well," replied Yvette in her I'm-your-mother voice. "In fact, you look absolutely worn out. You've got bags under your eyes."

Jean-Luc laughed. "It's two o'clock in the morning here, Mother."

Yvette looked shocked. "Two o'clock! But you should be in bed. Surely there is a time for lights out—"

"Yes," Jean-Luc said, "normally there is. But we're beginning a short holiday, and for the next few days, the rules will be relaxed. I can sleep as late as I care to tomorrow, so don't worry about me."

Yvette sighed. "You called at this time because you knew Maurice would be in the fields, didn't you?"

Shaking his head but smiling, Jean-Luc said, "You know me through and through, Mother."

"He would like to speak to you," Yvette said. "He misses you terribly."

"I miss him, too," replied Jean-Luc. "And Robert, and Louis, and everyone in the village. But you most of all. Is Father—is he happy?"

Yvette's expression grew serious. "Yes," she said quietly. "Yes, I really think he is. He has agreed to let Robert go on his little visit to Alkalurops, after all. And although the vineyard keeps him working hard, he loves what he is doing. I even think he's a little proud that he can run the vineyard alone for a while."

"I'm glad for Robert," said Jean-Luc. His brother had a wonderful opportunity to travel off-world and study wine-growing techniques on a distant agricultural planet, almost an agricultural university in itself. Jean-Luc had feared that his leaving for Starfleet Academy, over his father's strongest objections, had destroyed Robert's chances of making that trip. "Well," Jean-Luc said after a pause, "what's the news, Mother? I want to know about everything that's happened!"

For the better part of an hour they talked, and then Yvette had to go. It was time to prepare a meal for Maurice, and as always, she did all the cooking herself, not using replicators or other modern conveniences. "Good-bye, Son," Yvette said fondly. "Be sure to get some sleep, please."

"I will," promised Jean-Luc. "What are you cooking? No, wait, don't tell me. I wouldn't have the heart to stay here at the Academy if I started to think about your wonderful meals!"

"You're just like your father," Yvette said with a laugh. "He was always a flatterer, too. But we're just having an ordinary lunch, that's all."

Jean-Luc said, "It will be ambrosia compared to the food they serve here. Take my word for it."

They said their good-byes, and Jean-Luc went to bed just before three o'clock—or 0300, as he had grown accustomed to thinking of time at the Academy. He dreamed that he was home on the vineyard again, and in his dream the meal his mother served was the best one he had ever eaten.

He woke up late the next morning, jumped out of bed in a panic, and then remembered that it was a holiday. He felt better, though still lonely. And the memory of his dream meal made him ravenous. Jean-Luc had lunch in the first-year wing of the cadet dining hall. It was strange to sit in the large room almost alone. Only a few other cadets remained on campus—a few aliens, Vulcans and Andorians, the odd Betazoid, a dozen or so other species, sitting in small exclusive groups at the widely scattered tables. The only other human cadets were the haggard, desperate strugglers who needed every spare moment to study, cram, and practice. Even this early in the term they were beginning to be a weary-looking crew. Jean-Luc reflected that before long a good many of them would give up, drop out, and drift away.

It was a depressing thought, and he didn't want to talk to anyone about it. That was just as well, for he knew only a few of the remaining cadets, none of them as friends. He and his roommate, Jomo, were getting to know each other better, but even he had fled the campus for a quick visit home, so Jean-Luc was alone and restless. After lunch he went for a solitary walk through the campus. It was a bright, breezy day, not cold but cool, and he walked with his head down, smelling the faint salty odor of sea air. A curl of paper rolled across the walk in front of him, and without breaking stride, Jean-Luc stooped and snatched it up.

It was nothing, just a scribbled note about some topics that some upperclassman was researching in the library databanks. It was the kind of thing a student might carelessly drop without even realizing it. Jean-Luc crumpled the paper and tossed it into a recycler.

"Good for you!"

Jean-Luc looked around in surprise. A man knelt beside the walk some distance behind him, a thin, white-haired man wearing a plain gray jumpsuit and gloves. A large red watering can stood on the edge of the walkway next to his knees. He was using a trowel to scoop out a hole in the earth, and beside him lay a dozen clipped rose plants, their short branches bare and their roots encased in balls of earth. The man pointed with his trowel toward the recycling bin. "I like neat cadets. Especially those who take the time to pick up someone else's litter."

Jean-Luc approached him. "My father never liked litter, either," he said. "My brother and I can't just let it lie. What kind of rose sets are those?"

"Parisian," the man replied. "Something the Academy horticulturists bred. It's an interesting rose, a clear pink hybrid with transparent petals. Aroma's nice, too." He tilted his head and squinted up at Jean-Luc. "Why don't you have your hair trimmed?"

Suddenly self-conscious, Jean-Luc swept his hand through his thick brown hair. It had grown a bit shaggy since the first days of September. "I haven't had time. I'm a first-year cadet. Jean-Luc Picard."

"Call me Boothby," the man told him. "I've been the groundskeeper here for—well, never mind how long. Let's just say that I've been around awhile." He picked up one of the rose sets and tried it out in the hole he had dug. To Jean-Luc it looked like a tight fit, perhaps a little too tight.

"Is that hole big enough?" asked Jean-Luc.

"Isn't it?"

Jean-Luc shrugged. "Well, I don't know much about roses, but my father has made me plant a few hundred thousand grapevines. He'd never let me get away with digging a hole that small."

Boothby pulled the rose set back out of the earth and offered the trowel. "Here you are. I'm always willing to learn. Show me how you would do it."

Jean-Luc knelt and started to work. The earth turned easily, its rich, loamy smell reminding Jean-Luc of long afternoons spent on the vineyard. Soon he had dug a hole twice the diameter of the one Boothby had made. Jean-Luc settled back on his heels and grunted in satisfaction. "There," he said. "Now, if this were for a grapevine, I'd pour some water in—"

Boothby gestured to the watering can. "It's full, so be my guest."

Jean-Luc lifted the heavy watering can and poured a couple of inches of water into the depression he had made. Then he reached for the rose set, placed the root ball in the center of the little pool, and began to press the loose earth back around the roots. Boothby helped, patting the earth down, giving the stem an experimental tug to make sure it was firmly planted. "That's right," he said. "Plenty of room for the roots to spread, lots of support for the stem."

Jean-Luc laughed. "You never meant to plant the bush in that little hole. You were testing me."

"And you passed. Not many cadets know anything about growing plants and their needs. You did a good job, Mr. Picard."

"Thank you, sir."

Boothby snorted. "Don't call me 'sir.' I'm no Starfleet

officer. I happen to work for a living. Just Boothby will be fine." He pushed himself up and stretched. "Now, if you were in charge of this little job, where would you place the next one, Mr. Picard?"

"Just Jean-Luc will be fine." He pointed with the trowel. "There."

"I agree. Do it."

Together they planted a whole bed full of the roses, a triangular wedge between three of the walkways. At the end of the task Boothby stepped back, took a long look, and nodded his approval. "By the time you graduate, this will be a beautiful corner of the campus. When you come back as a commander to address a convocation, you can impress all the first-year cadets by telling them you did this."

"If I ever do graduate," Jean-Luc said, his tone gloomy.

"I think I recognize a bad case of first-year jitters," Boothby observed.

"Worse than that."

"Carry the watering can for me. Well, I'm as good a listener as I am a groundskeeper—and I happen to be a terrific groundskeeper. Come along with me, give me a hand with a few other little jobs, and tell me all about it."

Jean-Luc helped Boothby with a half-dozen other chores that day, and to his surprise he found himself talking to the old man (for by this time he was thinking of Boothby as pretty ancient) with an openness that he could never achieve with his father. He spoke of his brother, Robert, of his mother, Yvette, and most of all of stubborn, proud Maurice.

He even confessed that he had failed the first time he applied to the Academy—something he had never mentioned to anyone else, something that was his darkest secret. Through it all Boothby nodded and looked thoughtful and never once offered a suggestion.

"So," Jean-Luc concluded at the end of the day, "I suppose the real problem is that I'm terrified of failing. I was always the best. Champion runner, champion debater, valedictorian. But now there's Roger Wells. He's always going to be better than I am, and he's always going to rub it in. That's hard to take."

Boothby closed up the maintenance shed where they had stored the gardening tools. "Well," he said, "you haven't asked my advice, so I won't give you any. I will tell you, though, that those roses you helped me with wouldn't survive in France. Funny that they gave them a French name. They're best for this soil and this climate. And that's true of every growing thing, Jean-Luc. For every plant, the key to success is finding the right soil and the right climate. After that, everything else is easy."

Jean-Luc stared at him. "What?"

"Think it over. Take some time. You're young yet. You've got your whole life ahead of you." Boothby paused. "Have I missed any clichés?"

Jean-Luc laughed. "How about 'When I was your age'?"

Boothby gave him a long look. "Nope. I don't think I was ever your age, Jean-Luc. I was born a few years older than you are now. Sorry." They came to a branch in the walkway. Boothby looked up at the evening sky. The sun was setting, and twilight coming on. "I understand the Nova crews are going to be interesting this year," he said. "Good luck when you join them, Jean-Luc."

"If I join them," Jean-Luc said. "You don't know how hard the competition is."

"That's right. How would I know anything? I'm only a groundskeeper."

"No, I didn't mean that. I—"

"I'm not offended," Boothby said. "But I do hear things. Good listeners do. Good luck, Jean-Luc."

Their handshake was a little grimy, but Jean-Luc returned to his dorm feeling better than he had in days. Whatever happened, it seemed he had at least one friend on the Academy campus.

He wasn't alone, after all.

CHAPTER

4

The four-day weekend came to a close. Jean-Luc thought it had seemed more like two weeks. Funny how he had not managed to study quite as much as he had intended and how the Academy was still such a struggle afterward.

But he had to admit that in some ways life was better. He and Marta now studied together occasionally, and in addition to his roommate Jomo, Jean-Luc was beginning to make friends around the campus. He was even able to relax a bit now and then, and he discovered that his talent for playing cards made him fairly popular. That surprised him, since he took his abilities for granted. Perhaps, he thought, he had inherited a gene for being a cardsharp—both Maurice and Robert were fierce bridge and poker players. At any rate, during his rare evenings of relaxation, Jean-Luc began to acquire a reputation as a canny, cool bridge partner.

A few days after the long weekend Jean-Luc returned to his room, exhausted and ready for bed, after a satisfying session of cutthroat bridge in the student lounge. He yawned until his jaw creaked, and he barely muttered a greeting to his roommate as he pulled off his tunic. Jomo, who was lying in his bunk reading a book displayed on a data padd, glanced up with a grin. "Well, well," he said. "Hail the conquering hero. Congratulations, roomie. Well done."

Standing in his trousers and undershirt, Jean-Luc gave an elaborate bow. "Thank you, thank you, my adoring public. Now may I ask why you are congratulating me?"

"You don't know?" Jomo bounced up in bed, laughing. "It's all you've been talking about for weeks, and you really don't know?"

Throwing himself onto his bunk, Jean-Luc said, "Obviously not, but if you want to make it a big mystery, go right ahead."

Jomo manipulated his data padd. "It's on the announcement board. Has been there since 1700 hours, as you would know if you hadn't been wasting time with that silly game. Just a second, let me call it up . . . there. Read it and don't weep, you lucky dog."

Jean-Luc took the padd that Jomo offered. The screen displayed the usual menu of announcements, events schedules, and homework assignments for the various courses. Frowning, Jean-Luc read down the list until his eye stopped at one line: "Nova Command Teams Announced."

His finger trembling, Jean-Luc touched the screen to expand the heading into a full announcement. It swelled to fill the screen:

Nova Command Teams Announced
The following cadets have been assigned to Nova trainer crews. They will receive further orders within the next two days.

Lots and lots of upperclassmen . . . then a shorter list of first- and second-year cadets—ah, there it was! Jean-Luc's heart leaped. His name glowed at him from the screen. "I made it," he whispered.

"I say again, congratulations. I envy you—even though I knew I didn't have a chance this year. Oh, well, if I can ever learn enough physics, maybe next year."

Jean-Luc sat up on his bunk. He read the list again and again. He had made it, and there was Marta's name—he grinned foolishly at that—and his good humor could not even be wrecked when he saw that Roger Wells was on the list, also. Only six first-year cadets in all, and he was one of them!

He jumped out of bed and ran into the hallway. "I made it!" he shouted. "I'm on a Nova Command team!"

From the dorm rooms came a confusion of voices: "Who's that?"

"Lucky you!"

"Give me a break!"

Then a louder voice than all the others: "It's Jean-Luc Picard, the card-playing wonder. We're overjoyed, Jean-Luc. Now let us go to sleep!"

On a cool Friday morning the Nova Command cadets reported to the Clarke Conference Center, where they filled a small lecture hall. Jean-Luc's excitement had hardly faded in the days since the initial announcement, and he came in well ahead of time, walking into the hall in the wake of four serious fourth-year cadets, two of them Vulcans. Jean-Luc listened to their emotionless comments on the probabilities of acquiring valuable knowledge while assigned to the Nova Command. He had to fight the urge to break into a silly grin.

Pausing at the back of the hall, Jean-Luc saw a familiar figure sitting about halfway down. Approaching, he said, "Hello, Mr. Franklin. Mind if I sit here?"

The sandy-haired fencer looked around with a smile. "Ah, Mr. Picard. You can only sit there if you call me Tom and let me call you Jean-Luc. Congratulations on making the Nova team this year—not many of you first-year folks made it. Thought any more about fencing?"

With a laugh, Jean-Luc settled into a seat next to Franklin and immediately twisted halfway around so he could keep an eye on the entrance. "I won't have time for fencing or running for a while. I hope I can keep my place on the JV track team. Two weeks in space, and we still have to keep up with our studies!"

"Oh? Would you rather pass on the Nova invitation?"

"Not a chance." Jean-Luc craned his neck as a small crowd of cadets came in.

Franklin turned and looked, too. "What's up?"

"Nothing. I'm just expecting someone, that's all."

With a chuckle, Franklin said, "From the way you were staring, I thought perhaps we were being invaded by Denebian Slime Devils. Who are you looking for?"

Jean-Luc gave him an embarrassed smile. "Well, I know a couple of the other first-year cadets. Uh, Roger Wells and Marta Batanides. I thought maybe they might want to sit with us, that's all." He didn't want to admit that he rather hoped Marta would be alone. The day after they got their assignments, they had sort of dated— or, at least they had shared a meal to celebrate their good luck in making the Nova team. But Jean-Luc didn't want to jinx his chances by talking about Marta. He also didn't want to talk about Roger, so he tried to think of some other topic. Clearing his throat, Jean-Luc asked, "Uh, what's your academic specialty, Mr.—I mean, Tom?"

"Computer systems and artificial intelligence," Franklin said. "I'm hoping to complete the Science track and be assigned to a deep-space research vessel as an analyst and data specialist. How about you?"

Jean-Luc shook his head. "Well, since we don't have to commit until midway through second year, I haven't decided on any one track yet. But I'm leaning toward Science, too, since I like math and physics. I just haven't made up my mind about—look, there's Marta." He stood up and waved.

44

The dark-haired Marta saw him, waved back, and hurried to sit beside him. Jean-Luc introduced her to Tom Franklin, and the two had just said hello when Roger Wells came in, bragging loudly about something.

Marta rolled her eyes. "What an egotist," she whispered to Jean-Luc.

Jean-Luc, remembering how he had yelled in the hallway outside his dorm room, blushed to the roots of his hair. Fortunately, a trim, fit-looking man stepped up to the lectern at that moment, saving him from having to answer Marta.

"Good morning, cadets," the newcomer said. He wore the uniform of a Starfleet captain on active duty. He had a broad forehead, a thin face, twinkling blue eyes, and a small explosion of white hair. "I am Captain W. G. Page, and I will be your commanding officer while you are detached to Nova Command duty. First, I want to congratulate you on making the team. You have all demonstrated exceptional ability, and you should be proud of your achievement. Second, I want to warn you that Nova Command teams are hard work—but you should be used to that by now."

Captain Page went on to explain that the cadets were to report to the shuttle landing pads early the following day. They would be divided into thirty flight teams of five members each—five was the minimum safe complement for flying a Nova trainer. The teams would be flown from the Academy to Bradbury Orbital Base, the Martian orbiting station where they would undergo a week of simulation training. Each team would then receive individual orders for a real mission, flown on their own without direct Starfleet aid. After the mission, each team would have two days of evaluation to see what they had learned from the experience.

"Then," Captain Page finished, "you will return to San Francisco, where you will have one whole day off before resuming your studies. And I'm sure no one will be behind."

Someone snickered, and the captain raised an eyebrow at the unlucky cadet. "Oh, you thought that was funny, Mr. Redderly? From now on," he said in a dry voice, "I'll be sure to tell you when I've made a joke."

"It's gorgeous," Marta whispered to Jean-Luc.

Jean-Luc could only nod. Before them hovered a half-sized hologram of a Nova Command trainer. It was a sleek little craft, with one small engine nacelle and a half-circular command and quarters section. The hologram made the little ship glow a brilliant white, all except for the registration number and the name of the craft—in this case, the *Aldebaran*—in red numerals and letters, aft of the leading edge. It looked a little like a spacegoing stingray.

Captain Page was speaking in the darkness, describing the capabilities of the trainer. "The engine is a standard Stevens thruster, capable of point five warp speed," he was saying. "You may notice that the Nova design is very similar to the mineralogical scout ships used to examine asteroid fields in other systems. It has a strong forward shield so you cadets won't bump into anything, and about the only difference between the trainer and the scout is that the scout has warp two capability. You won't need to travel faster than light-speed, however, since none of you will be leaving the solar system—we hope." He paused. "That was a joke."

Everyone laughed dutifully.

"Sir?" asked a voice that Jean-Luc recognized as that of Roger Wells. "I understand the scout craft are armed with a single phaser for destroying asteroids. How about the trainers?"

"We don't want you shooting up our asteroids, cadet," the captain said. "No armament. And you might be interested to know that scouts generally use their phasers for dissection, not destruction. Sometimes they need to cut an asteroid in half to see what it is made of."

The hologram became a schematic, showing a cutaway view of the trainer. "You will notice, however," the captain continued, "that the trainer has one or two modern conveniences. You have both attractor and repulsor tractor beams. That is so you can push an asteroid out of the way if necessary, Mr. Wells." On the schematic a small area aft of the command bridge lit up. "And you have a three-person transporter station here."

He went on to show the stations aboard the craft: The center chair was the captain's station, of course. And, as the captain said before Roger could ask, an upper-class cadet would be the captain of each vessel. The executive officer sat to the left of the captain and would be in charge of transporter, tractor-beam operation, and life support. Behind and to the right of the captain was the science station. The science officer on each craft would double as the astronavigator. To the left of that station was the computer operations and communications center. And finally, to the left of that was the engineering station and helm, from where the engineer would steer the ship.

"Even though one of you will be the captain," concluded Captain Page, "I remind you that you are part of a team. In the next weeks, get to know your teammates very well. You will have to trust and depend on them, and they on you. Remember, space is a very cold, dark, and unforgiving place. A mistake there could cost the lives of your friends and of yourself. That, cadets, is not a joke."

And no one laughed.

Marta Batanides and Jean-Luc were strolling in Golden Gate Park, looking at the bridge, lighted like multiple strings of jewels. Jean-Luc took a deep breath of the damp, cool air. "It's the first time I've been off-campus since the term began."

"There's an operetta tonight at the Bay Center Theater. Want to go?"

"What is it?"

"A classic. Gilbert and Sullivan's *H.M.S. Pinafore.*"

Jean-Luc made a face. "Do you really want to go?"

"Well—yes, I do. What's wrong?"

Heaving a great sigh, Jean-Luc said, "Nothing, but every time Roger Wells scores over me, he has to remind me of his British heritage. And that's a British play. Now, if it were a French opera—"

Marta hit him playfully on the arm. "You're just being silly. All right, if you won't go with me, maybe I'll just look up Roger."

"I'll go, I'll go!" Jean-Luc said. "Only promise me that afterward we can go to a French restaurant. Maybe Wellington beat Napoleon at Waterloo, but a French chef can defeat a British cook anytime."

"It's a deal," Marta said. "And anyway, a good restaurant meal will have to be better than dining-hall food."

The stars were coming out. Marta, looking up, pointed out Venus, low in the west, shimmering just over the horizon. Higher, closer to the zenith, was the glowing white point of Vega. "You can't see the Centauri stars from here," she said. "Only in the Southern Hemisphere. It feels funny to be so far from home."

"I can imagine," Jean-Luc replied, reflecting that in a way he was farther from home than she. At least if she wanted to return to her family for a visit, she would not face a father who would try to keep her there! "Marta, you've been in space before. What was it like?"

She laughed. "I've told you that story. It was like a crazy ride at an amusement park—but then, I took a knockabout old liner. It's going to be different in a trainer." Her shoulder bumped his. "A trainer is so small. And space is so vast and black."

Jean-Luc felt her shiver. "Are you frightened?" he asked in surprise.

She took a moment before answering. "Not exactly. But think of all that could go wrong."

He put his arm around her. "Nothing will go wrong. We're too good for that."

"Now you sound like Roger."

"Ouch!" yipped Jean-Luc. "Cut to the bone! Come along, girl. Let's go see your ridiculous operetta so that we can then have some decent food. And as for the dangers of space—well, what do I always say?"

They said it in unison: "We'll see about that!" And they both broke into laughter.

CHAPTER

5

The Nova Command teams were slated for departure very early the next morning—so early, in fact, that Jean-Luc reported before the sun was up. He carried a single suitcase and his data padd, the only luggage he would be allowed to take with him on the long trip. The departure order glowing on his padd told him he was to board Shuttle 6, one of the second flight groups to lift off. Marta, looking just as excited as he felt, was to board that shuttle, too, so they stood together, skin tingling a little in the predawn chill.

Jean-Luc's heart was fluttering. He had flown before, a good number of times in fact. When he was in high school, he had taken a number of trips to North America, Australia, and all over Europe on various school excursions and competitions. And of course he had taken the trans-Atlantic shuttle from France to San Francisco to begin his career at Starfleet Academy.

Still, all of those flights had been suborbital trips. He had only approached the fringes of space. This time he would really be out there, in the dark interplanetary reaches between Earth and Mars. Just knowing that this trip would be the real thing, not a holographic simulation, made him shiver with anticipation.

Five shuttle pads were operating. With a hum of engines and a whine of power, the first flight of five took off, and five more Starfleet Type 12 Personnel Shuttles settled onto the pads. The boarding light changed from red to green, the automatic gate of Pad 1 opened, Jean-Luc hefted his bag, and he and Marta hurried aboard. Two Starfleet lieutenants watched as the cadets filed in, went down the center aisle, and found seats. When everyone was aboard, one of them said, "You've boarded Interplanetary Shuttlecraft *Olympus*. In just a moment we'll lift off. We expect to leave the Earth's atmosphere in twenty minutes. While in low orbit, we will proceed with thrusters to Departure Point Gamma. Then we will engage warp drive for the trip to Mars. Our warp transit time should be four hours and twenty minutes, and we anticipate docking at 1300 hours, standard time. Any questions?"

"No, Lieutenant—we just want to get off the ground!" yelled someone from up ahead.

Jean-Luc winced. It was Roger Wells's voice. Just his luck to be stuck on a shuttle with that particular cadet! At least Roger was five rows ahead, in the very front of the cabin. And at least Marta was here beside him in the back row, and a row ahead of him sat Tom Franklin. With luck, Roger might not even notice Jean-Luc. Maybe the flight wouldn't be all that bad.

Jean-Luc had chosen a window seat. He stared out as the shuttle lifted off and began the long arc of its climb to space. Acceleration pressed him back in the seat until the ship's artificial gravity cut in, a minute or so after takeoff. They headed east, and the sunrise caught them before long. Jean-Luc could see orange-yellow deserts, snaky green riverbeds, huge masses and splotches of low clouds far below the shuttle. The sky grew a darker and darker blue until it was violet. The misty blue horizon began to show a definite curve. Stars appeared, and before Jean-Luc knew it, the shuttle was in low Earth orbit. The black vacuum of space, strewn with stars, was overhead and all around the shuttle. He stared down as the eastern seaboard of North America slipped away, looking like a continent sketched on a globe.

"Look, Jean-Luc. No, not down. Look up." Marta pointed out a starship, an enormous Excelsior-class vessel, in a slightly higher orbit. "Going to McKinley," she said.

Jean-Luc nodded. McKinley Station was where Starfleet ships went for refitting and repair. He wondered if they would get a glimpse of it.

As it turned out, they would not. "Cadets," one of the pilots said over the intercom, "we are about to engage the warp drive. If this is new to you, you'd better hold on tight. Here we go!"

Involuntarily Jean-Luc gripped the armrests of his seat. Marta laughed, and all around him experienced space travelers were giggling at the reactions of their less knowledgeable friends. The cochrane engines throbbed a little louder, the starfield outside blurred . . . and that was all. With the inertia damping field of a shuttlecraft providing gravity for him, Jean-Luc didn't even have a sensation of accelerating. He relaxed. "I should have known better than that. They caught me off guard."

"It's an old tradition," Marta said.

Tom Franklin turned around and rested his hand on the back of his seat. "So far, so good," he said with a smile. "Enjoying the trip, Jean-Luc?"

"Immensely."

Marta said, "I'll enjoy it more when I find out about our assignments. I don't want to wind up being the communications officer!"

"Oh, you won't," Franklin said. "You're to be the chief engineer and helmsman on the *Ishtar*. I'm handling communications and computer operations."

Jean-Luc gave him a suspicious stare. "I didn't think assignments would be announced until we arrived."

Franklin grinned and shrugged. "I told you I'm interested in artificial intelligence and computer systems. It so happens that I helped design the program that made the team assignments. I thought you two might like to be on the same ship, and since you're good company, I decided to tag along as well. We'll be shipmates aboard the good trainer *Ishtar*."

"Oh." Jean-Luc hesitated, but he couldn't hold the question in: "And what will my assignment be?"

"You're holding the navigation and science seat."

Jean-Luc tried to keep a smile on his face, but he didn't quite succeed. Marta noticed his disappointment and asked, "What's wrong? That's a great assignment."

"Oh, it is," said Jean-Luc. "It's just that—well, I know that a Nova trainer must be commanded by a fourth-year cadet, so I had no illusions about being captain. But I hoped maybe I might be the executive officer."

Franklin shook his head. "Sorry, Jean-Luc. You were in the running, but Roger Wells edged you out."

"What?"

Franklin blinked at the irritation in Jean-Luc's voice. "Uh-oh. Did I make a mistake?"

Marta said, "No, not really. It's just that we're surprised to be on the same ship with him."

"And not delighted," added Jean-Luc.

"Sorry," Franklin told them. "I thought you all knew each other. If I'd known—"

"Forget it," Jean-Luc said. "It's all water under the bridge now. Roger's the exec. But tell me, who's the captain to be?"

Franklin straightened and looked up ahead. "Tabath Ran. I can see the back of her head from here. She's sitting next to Roger. Do you know her?"

Both Jean-Luc and Marta shook their heads.

"I'm not surprised," Franklin said. "She's a Kemoran, and you've probably noticed how they keep to themselves."

Jean-Luc had glimpsed two or three Kemoran cadets—the alien students tended to go about in couples or small groups. They were stumpy humanoids, all of them more than a head shorter than Jean-Luc. Kemora, their home world, had a heavy gravity, a very salty, shallow planetary ocean, and a single continent, hot and dry. Kemorans were a semi-amphibian species, comfortable on dry land but able to stay submerged for long periods. They were somewhat lizardlike in appearance, their skin covered with iridescent hexagonal scales. These shone in all the colors of the rainbow, depending on the light. Their eyes were slitted and red, and they had no real noses, just a flat pad with four thin nostrils. Their mouths, by contrast, were well-developed. In fact, their lips stretched from ear to ear—or would have, if Kemorans had external ears. Boys and girls dressed alike, even when they weren't wearing Starfleet Academy uniforms. Their normal clothing consisted of odd-shaped boots, which gave them the appearance of having feet like ducks, and one-piece silvery jumpsuits. In addition, both sexes were bald, and Jean-Luc couldn't tell the females from the males. Of course, he had barely spoken to any of the clannish Kemorans.

"They're rare in Starfleet," he said.

Franklin nodded. "Only about a hundred Kemorans in the service right now. Only six of them at the Academy. Tabath Ran is one of the most gifted upper-class cadets, or so I hear. She tends to be a little gruff and a little grumpy, but don't sell her short. She's a first-rate pilot, and she'll insist on running a tight ship."

*　　*　　*

Jean-Luc had never seen anything as beautiful as Bradbury Orbital Base. The shuttle had dropped out of warp speed a few hundred thousand kilometers short of Mars, and they approached the planet using only thrusters. They were coming straight in from the sun, so Mars swelled into a huge tawny-red sphere, pockmarked with ancient craters, studded with enormous volcanoes, and— now that the process of terraforming was well under way—blurred with the blue haze of an oxygen atmosphere and striped by long white swatches of cloud.

Bringing water and oxygen from outer bodies of the solar system for generations, humans had been busily changing the face of the dead planet. Beneath his tunic, on a chain around his neck, Jean-Luc wore an ancient St. Christopher medallion. It was a family heirloom, supposedly brought back from Jerusalem during a crusade in the Middle Ages by a remote ancestor.

But somewhat closer in time, one Auguste Picard, Jean-Luc's great-great grandfather, had worn it to Mars and back. Jean-Luc had heard a little family talk about his illustrious ancestor, but not much—because Maurice Picard seemed to regard even that remote space-traveler somehow a traitor to the cause of vineyards and grapes. At the Academy, Jean-Luc had run across the name in history texts, and it intrigued him to learn that Auguste Picard was an early settler on Mars, living under a dome on the surface, long before the terraforming process that had made Mars habitable and that was still going on at this very moment.

Jean-Luc shivered a little. He was taking his great-grandfather's medallion on a homecoming trip of a sort. He knew that Auguste Picard had died long before efforts had made it possible for anyone to venture outside a pressurized Martian dome. What would he think of his planet if he could see it now, as his great-great grandson did? Jean-Luc resolved to find the time to go down to the Martian surface at least once, to go for a low-gravity walk out in the open, under the Martian sky. It would be a kind of tribute to that older Picard, his fellow space-traveler.

But right now, Jean-Luc couldn't get enough of the sight of the planet as it grew larger with their approach. Where would he take his walk? Probably down in the great Mariner rift valley. At the lower elevations the atmosphere was already thick enough for humans to breathe without masks, and in the huge rift valley, named for an unmanned space probe that had landed on Mars centuries ago, a real sea was already rippling in the sun. Auguste Picard's dream was coming true. One day Mars would be a smaller brother to Earth, and that day was fast approaching.

Jean-Luc gasped. His view of the planet was splendid, breathtaking. But what had really taken his breath was the moment that Bradbury Station swept into view, sailing serenely from behind the curved, atmosphere-blurred horizon of Mars. The orbital station was a shining white, a complex of six enormous work and habitation disks, each level capable of supporting more than ten thousand colonists and workers. It was far larger than either of the two puny moons of Mars, and as the shuttle approached, it grew until it more than filled the viewports. Still they were a long way away, and Jean-Luc could see the tiny specks of two- and three-person shuttles and the barely visible darting forms of one-person work bees, the tiny ships that carried out the ordinary tasks of maintaining and enlarging one of the solar system's largest space constructs.

"Close your mouth, farm boy," came a sneering voice behind him. "Your tongue will dehydrate!"

Jean-Luc glanced around in annoyance, his mood

ruined. Roger stood there, leaning on Marta's seat back. Roger was not a welcome visitor. "Sorry if my enthusiasm offends you, but it's the first time I've seen a working space station," Jean-Luc said.

Roger patted Marta on the shoulder. "Our wine-growing friend is a little naive, isn't he?"

Marta didn't look up at him. "I was dazzled when I first went into space, too, Roger."

Roger grinned. "Oh, so was I. . . . I think. Of course, I can't really remember—I was probably about two years old at the time. After we dock, why don't we get a bite to eat together? I'll tell you about it."

Marta gave him an irritated glare. "Thank you, Roger, but Jean-Luc and I already have plans." She turned to Jean-Luc, giving him a wink. "Isn't that right?"

"Absolutely," Jean-Luc said. He fought hard to keep his poker face on, though the way Marta had just put Roger in his place delighted him.

Roger sniffed and straightened up. "All right," he said. Then, in a louder voice, he added, "I guess second-raters just like to hang out together, that's all."

Jean-Luc's cheeks grew hot. He could stand being teased about almost anything else, but not about that. "Go away," he growled. Marta put her hand on his arm and gave him a little warning squeeze: *Be careful,* it told Jean-Luc silently.

"Oh, I'm going," Roger said. "We have to strap in for docking, you know. But let me tell you something, Mr. Picard. As executive officer on the *Ishtar,* I'm going to be in charge of reporting on crew morale and achievement. You'd better shape up if you want to get a good rating." Suddenly he grinned and gave Marta an extravagant wink, as though his threat were just a joke. He went forward.

As he passed Tom Franklin, Franklin turned in his seat. He had a worried expression on his face. He silently mouthed the word "Sorry" to Jean-Luc.

Marta patted his arm. "Don't let him get to you. Roger's so full of himself, he doesn't have any room left over for manners."

"I know," Jean-Luc returned. "It isn't just that he's good. I could accept that. It's that he's so blasted smug about it!"

Just then the pilot asked everyone to prepare for docking. Jean-Luc turned and stared out the window again. By now the only thing he could see was a gigantic landing bay, with several shuttles already down. He stared as they slipped through the forcefield-protected space lock, felt the little sickening lurch as the shuttle gravity gave way to the station gravity, and heard the metallic *clang* as the shuttle set down.

He drew a deep breath. What he had said to Marta was true, as far as it went. But what really bothered him, down deep, was the suspicion that in his younger days in high school, he had been a lot like Roger. Always the best at everything, and not afraid to let people know about his accomplishments. Never a moment of doubt—until his first humiliating failure when he applied to Starfleet Academy. Had he possibly been as irritating as Roger could be? Jean-Luc hoped not, but he half suspected that many of his acquaintances had felt the same dull resentment for him that he now felt for Roger.

Oh, well, Jean-Luc was over his cockiness now, at least on the inside. He still kept up appearances of assurance, and he still tried to be a very cool and collected customer, but the truth was that he no longer felt the calm attitude he projected. Now he was just pretending to have a great deal more confidence than he actually had.

Jean-Luc thought grimly that the Nova Command would be a chance for him to show what he could do. He ground his teeth together. He'd show Roger! He'd show all of them!

The hatchway opened at the rear, and he and Marta rose together. They stepped out of the shuttle and into the first real challenge of their lives at Starfleet Academy.

CHAPTER

6

"Congratulations, Cadet Picard," said Captain Page dryly. "You've just scrambled Mr. Franklin's molecules. Let's see if he comes out as a purple giraffe."

Jean-Luc Picard ground his teeth. It was hardly fair—this was his first time trying to operate a transporter, after all—but then no one had promised him that the Academy would be easy. He looked at the monitor. Tom Franklin grinned at him and waved. It was an eerie sort of wave, since Tom was missing everything from his arm-pits down. His head and shoulders simply floated in air, looking ghostly and weird.

"You're lucky it's just a holographic simulation," Captain Page told Jean-Luc. "Otherwise, you'd be hours cleaning up the transporter pad." He readjusted the transporter controls, and the image of Franklin became whole again. "Now, what's the first thing to do after you've locked on to a target?"

"Activate the pattern buffer," Jean-Luc said.

"Exactly right. Next time, do that before you engage the transporter beam, and then perhaps you won't cut your target into tiny little pieces."

Jean-Luc concentrated. It was one thing to know all about transporter theory and technology, but it was another to actually be at the controls. Simple and automated as they were, they still gave a hapless cadet a vast range of mistakes to make, as he had just proved in a spectacular fashion.

When Jean-Luc had run the transporter program correctly several times, gaining speed with each repetition, Captain Page grunted his satisfaction. "All right, let's try the real thing." He told the computer to switch off the simulation override. "I'm not sure I'd trust you quite yet to transport me anywhere, Mr. Picard, so instead let me send you out to the *Ishtar* and back. Ever transported before?"

"Yes," Jean-Luc said.

"Into space?"

"No," he had to admit. "But I've used the short-range network on Earth several times."

"Well, this is the same principle," Page said. "However, in going from ship to ship, you may not have all the little conveniences of groundside transportation. Ever noticed how the ground stations give you a long exit corridor? That's to help adjust atmospheric pressure, temperature, and other variables. Starships are fairly standard, so you won't have that long corridor. But they're only *fairly* standard. So although we'll do some adjusting for small differences in atmosphere and pressure, you may find the sensations just a bit different. Get ready."

Jean-Luc stood on the round transporter pad. Seconds passed.

"Well?" Captain Page asked with exaggerated courtesy.

Jean-Luc swallowed. He had forgotten that the person being transported from a ship always gave the command, regardless of his or her rank. "Energize."

A whine of energy, high-pitched and rising in volume. His skin tingled. The scene before him—the small transporter bay with its three pads—sparkled and faded, and for a moment there was cool, empty blackness. Then sparkling lights again, and he materialized. His ears popped, not painfully, but enough for him to notice. He drew a deep breath and smelled the sharp scent of metal, the air cooler in his nostrils than he expected. The *Ishtar* was a small ship, the transporter bay much more cramped and crowded than the one he had just left on the station. His communicator badge chirped, and he touched it. "Picard here."

"How was the trip?" asked Page's voice.

"Very comfortable, thank you, sir."

"Of course. As long as you're there, you might as well go forward and inspect your science station. I'll give you ten minutes, then report back to the transporter bay for return here."

"Thank you, sir."

Jean-Luc walked through a narrow corridor. He had studied sketches and holos of the ship, and he already knew his way around. A hatch led down to the five cramped bunks, tiny bathroom, and small replicator galley of the crew quarters; ahead of him was the bridge. The *Ishtar* was docked, receiving its energy from the station instead of from its own power plants, but everything was working. The automatic doors hissed open as they sensed Jean-Luc's approach.

He walked onto the bridge. The forward viewscreen was blank at the moment. Jean-Luc looked around at the five seats. The *Ishtar* wasn't much as spaceships went. It couldn't attain warp speeds, it was unarmed, and its working space was constricted. But as he slid into his station beneath a projecting console, Jean-Luc felt nothing but elation. The *Ishtar* was, for the moment, anyway, *his* ship. He ran through a quick check of sensors and monitors and found everything ready. Then he got out of his seat, stooping to avoid bumping his head on the projecting bank of overhead consoles. After a moment of indecision, he went forward to the captain's seat and settled into that.

"Computer," he said on impulse. "Activate the viewscreen."

The screen came to life. He saw the *Ishtar* was tethered to a docking ring—in fact, if he opened the hatch to the living quarters and then opened the one below that, he would be in an airlock leading into the Bradbury Station. Transporting onto the ship instead of walking

aboard was just an option at this point. To his left and right, other training ships were docked. He could see the *Aphrodite* to his right, and beyond that the *Quetzalcoatl* and the *Ra*. Others lay too far away for him to see their names. One, far down the line, left its station and with a touch of thrusters moved off toward the darkness of space.

Jean-Luc envied that crew, already out for a short shake-down cruise. He sighed, ordered the computer to turn off the screens, and hurried back to the transporter bay. He had just stepped onto the pad when Captain Page's voice came over the communicator: "Standing by."

"Energize," Jean-Luc said smartly.

Again the shimmering moment of disorientation, and then he was back aboard the station, Captain Page smiling at him from behind the transporter controls. "Welcome back. I see you are in one piece."

"Yes, sir. It was a good trip. Thank you."

"You're welcome." Captain Page turned off the power of the transporter console, and then with a suspiciously bland smile, he asked, "By the way, Mr. Picard, how was the captain's seat?"

Jean-Luc blinked. "I—sir, I—how did you know?"

Page laughed. "I wouldn't think much of you if you didn't try it out for size." He stepped away from the transporter console and gave it a quick visual checkout. "Now come over here and see if you remember anything of what you've learned so far. You can start by turning on the power, if you can recall exactly which switch to use."

Not every session was one-on-one. Bradbury Station did not provide huge lecture halls, but one meeting room could accommodate up to seventy-five cadets. Jean-Luc attended lectures and presentations there, usually with Marta or Tom Franklin, sometimes with other navigation and science-specialist cadets. After one of these, as he and Tom were leaving the classroom, the sight of Marta walking beside Roger Wells surprised him. He hurried to catch up. "Hi," he said. "I didn't see you come in."

Marta returned his smile. "Roger and I got there a little late. We sat together in the back."

"Oh."

Roger took Marta's arm. "And we're going to do a little private studying now, Picard. I'm sure you've got some cramming to do to bring your science-officer skills up to par."

Jean-Luc glared at him. "Actually, I'm all caught up." Ignoring Roger, he turned back to Marta. "Free for dinner tonight?"

"Well, I sort of promised—"

"The two of us are dining together," Roger said. He tugged Marta's arm. "Come on, we don't want to be late."

Jean-Luc must have looked stricken. Marta gave him a worried glance and said quickly, "It's not what you think." Then she and Roger hurried away, losing themselves in the crowd.

Tom Franklin had kept discreetly out of the way during the exchange. He came up behind Jean-Luc. "I meant what I said on the shuttle. I really am sorry about tinkering with the assignments," he said in a low voice. "I didn't realize that you and Roger didn't get along."

"Forget it," Jean-Luc growled. He stalked out, angry and hurt. Instead of going to dinner, he reported to the computer-assisted learning lab, whose computer the cadets had come to call "Cal," after the initials of the lab. Jean-Luc slipped into a vacant booth and sat for a moment, his emotions steaming. So Marta was too busy for him, was she? Well, he could make himself just as busy as she was. Although he had finished all the work required of him for the day, nothing in the book said he couldn't get in some extra study. He could practice on his own, with a holographic simulator.

Then, he thought, *just wait until we're in space. Let her great friend Roger slip up once—just once!—and I'll show him up for the fool he is.* For a few moments Jean-Luc grinned fiercely as he imagined all sorts of ways that Roger could be humiliated. Then he realized that, pleasant as his fantasies were, they were only fantasies. He had to approach this task without anger, as—well, as Mr. Spock would have done. Vulcans controlled their emotions, made them secondary to the task that had to be done. Jean-Luc breathed deeply, trying to calm down.

When at last he had control of himself, he said, "Cal, I wish to review scanning and recording procedures for the *Ishtar* science probes. Class Nine simulation."

"Class Nine simulation," Cal's voice repeated. "Do you wish to assign speed?"

"No. Make it challenging."

The holographic representation of the *Ishtar*'s science section shimmered into existence. "Astronavigation," Cal said. "Give me a reading of position."

Jean-Luc slipped his fingers across the control board, calling up computer memory. "We are in a planetary system," he said. "Current position is one point five AU from the star. The star is a type F-Nine. We are in Alpha Quadrant, within fifty light-years of the solar system. Hold on—one class-M planet." In his computer screen, the image of the planet glowed, unearthly but holding an atmosphere that could support human life.

"Scan for life-forms."

Although he had no viewport with which to see it directly, the figures and the simulated displays told Jean-Luc about the simulated planet. Slightly more massive than Earth, slightly drier, with oceans covering some sixty-six percent of its surface, land masses another twenty-nine percent, and the remainder made up of polar ice caps. The slowly revolving image in his computer screen showed blood-red continents smudged with vast areas of purple-green terrain. The oceans were a brilliant emerald green.

"Nitrogen-oxygen atmosphere," Jean-Luc reported. "Life scan is in progress, but I'd guess that this world has a large plant biomass."

"Why so, Mr. Picard?"

"Because plants consume nitrogen and carbon dioxide

71

and produce oxygen. This planet has less nitrogen than Earth and more oxygen, so it's reasonable to assume that it has more plant life. Those purple areas may be huge expanses of ground plants."

Cal said, "You are right. Let us seek more information. Exact atmospheric composition?"

Jean-Luc studied his instruments. "Nitrogen makes up sixty-three percent, oxygen thirty percent, carbon dioxide two point four percent, water vapor one point seven two percent, inert gases . . ." He read out the list. A sensor chimed to let him know that a planetary scan had just been completed. "I'm getting direct life-form readings now."

"Report, please."

"No electromagnetic band activity—"

"Meaning no intelligent life, Mr. Picard?"

Jean-Luc frowned. "Not necessarily. It could mean that any intelligent life form simply is not using elecromagnetic communication—no radio, television, or holographic transmissions."

"That is a good point. Continue with your life-forms assessment."

Jean-Luc nodded. "According to the readouts, there should be only a minimal number of animal life-forms, but as I predicted, massive amounts of vegetation. It must be a jungle planet. Or perhaps the seas support a great deal of algae, seaweed, and similar plant forms."

"Preliminary conclusions?"

"A world in the early stages of evolution," Jean-Luc shot back. "Since an F-Nine sun is a short-lived star, this planet probably has not had much time to undergo evolution. I suggest it might be comparable to the Devonian period of Earth's development. Chances of sentient life near zero—wait."

"Report, Mr. Picard."

Jean-Luc studied his readouts. Something was wrong, subtly odd about the charts and graphs. He noticed a spike in the EM bandwidths that covered the old-fashioned radio-wave broadcast bands. "Odd. Now I'm getting a very localized reading of electromagnetic transmission. That wasn't there before."

"Can you localize the transmission, Mr. Picard?"

Jean-Luc frantically scanned the whole planetary surface. "Wait a bit—it isn't on the planet. It's coming from something in orbit."

Cal had him pinpoint the orbital anomaly. Their imaginary ship closed on it. "Report, Mr. Picard," said the relentless voice of Cal.

"It's a spaceship," Jean-Luc said. "Type unknown. Mass, one hundred seven thousand standard tons. No life-form readings. I can't find any plasma traces, no antimatter readings at all, no dilithium—it doesn't seem to have warp capability. It doesn't seem to be operational. The only energy reading I'm getting is that electromagnetic signal. Cal, request that Communications put the broadcast on screen."

In its remote voice, Cal said, "Communications reports that the signal contains no visual images. Audio only."

"Let's hear it."

The eerie, piping sounds of flute music filled Jean-

Luc's ears. Except that the flute played no melody and really wasn't a musical instrument. At times the sound went up the scale, becoming so shrill that it made Jean-Luc's teeth ache. Then it lost pitch and volume until it was a low thrumming vibration, felt rather than heard. "Is that communication?" Jean-Luc asked.

Cal wouldn't give a centimeter. "Is it communication, Mr. Picard?"

Jean-Luc checked to make sure the Universal Translator was operating correctly. According to the translator's diagnostic program, it was—which meant that this voice, if it was a voice, was not in the standard language-pattern banks. If an alien was speaking, it was an alien the Federation had never conversed with before. Jean-Luc began to feel uncomfortable. Something about this situation bothered him.

"I'm modifying the Universal Translator patterns," Jean-Luc said. "This sounds almost cetacean. I'm asking the communicator to extrapolate possible meanings based on whale song—"

The flute sound modulated, becoming more regular and breaking up into short bursts that almost sounded like words. A second EM spike showed up. "We're being scanned," Jean-Luc said. "It doesn't seem to be hostile, though—just checking us out, as we're checking it out. I recommend hailing the unknown ship, all frequencies, offering assistance."

"The communications officer follows your suggestion. The officer reports no response," Cal said at once.

"No life-forms," Jean-Luc said again, studying his instruments. His voice was low, thoughtful, and distinctly worried. "How can that be, if they're hailing us? Someone must be aboard that ship."

"Why?" asked Cal.

"Because someone's hailing us," Jean-Luc said. "But I can't determine what kind of life-form it could possibly be. Since the voice is a little like the song of dolphins or whales, I've checked for oceanic forms as well as land forms. I can find no energy patterns or—wait. Let me cross-check the translator signal against machine patterns. This might be an automatic message, a recording."

"Carry out your machine-pattern analysis," Cal said.

After another adjustment of the controls, Jean-Luc felt the hair prickling on the back of his neck. The fluting, piping sound had become an emotionless, high-pitched voice: ". . . have disregarded the warning, automatic defense systems have been engaged. Repeat: Surrender at once. Since you have disregarded—"

"Cal, raise shields! Get us out of here!" Jean-Luc roared.

"Is that your recommendation to the captain?"

"Yes!"

After a second Cal said, "There is a ninety percent probability that your captain will demand further explanation before consenting to—"

Everything went dark.

Jean-Luc pounded the edge of the desk in frustration. A moment later the lights in the booth came back up. "The alien craft swept the *Ishtar* with a powerful organic-destruction ray," Cal said in its curiously cheerful mechanical voice. "You and the other crew members have just been evaporated."

"What was it, Cal?"

"A dead warship. It drifted into this system thousands of years ago. It was sealed in a stasis field, so no deterioration of its weaponry or systems occurred. Your scans disrupted that field, causing the ship to become active. Even without a crew, the ship acted as a weapon of war and struck out against a potential threat."

Jean-Luc settled back, his face set in a grim mask of determination. "Very well. I made some mistakes. I won't make them again. Let's run another simulation. And then a few more, just for good measure."

He got better.

By the end of the session, he was bone-weary, still angry, and ravenously hungry after missing his dinner. But he had only died once.

It did not help to think that, out in the real dangers of space, once would have been enough.

CHAPTER

7

Cadet Captain Ran glared at her crew. She could not help that, not with her deep-set slitted red eyes and their overhanging ridges of bone that gave her a look of fury even when she was asleep. But this time she meant it. "No mistakes," she said. "Captain Page will be here in a minute to brief us on the mission. Whatever it is, I will tolerate no mistakes—from any of you. All of you seem to see this mission as a sort of game, but it is not. It's my chance to prove myself. You may not know that no Kemoran has ever commanded a Starfleet vessel. I intend to be the first, and—" She hesitated, the slits of her pupils widening momentarily. "And—and I will, uh, tolerate no mistakes. At ease!"

Jean-Luc relaxed. Tom Franklin stood to his right, Marta to his left, and beyond Marta, Roger Wells. Once again Jean-Luc felt alone and isolated. Oh, Franklin was always ready for a friendly chat or game of cards, but that was different, less like a friendship than his relationship with his older brother, Robert. No, what bothered him was Marta's cool attitude. They had never actually quarreled, but somehow their exchanges had become snappish and short.

And Jean-Luc couldn't help noticing, Roger stood closer to her than he did.

"Cadets, attention!" Tabath Ran's brisk command brought Jean-Luc's shoulders back, chin in.

Captain Page entered, glanced around, and nodded his satisfaction. "As you were, cadets. You may be seated." In a crisp voice he added, "Computer, lower the lights and prepare the holographic demonstration of Nova Command mission eight."

They all found seats around the long briefing table. As the lights went down, a holographic simulation of Mars, its two natural satellites, and Bradbury Station glimmered into visibility. "Just to orient you," Captain Page said. "Keep an eye on our location here. Computer, scale down."

The planet shrank to a red dot, a curving yellow line showing its orbital path. A haze appeared, millions of tiny glowing specks representing the asteroid belt. Here and there were small yellow X marks, showing the locations of asteroid mining centers. Jean-Luc sat near the red dot of Mars. Across the table from him, on the far side of the asteroid belt, a green circle glowed. It began to blink.

"Locate the Jovian LaGrange Station Voltaire," instructed Page. "It's the flashing green circle. Everyone got it? Computer, lay in the mission track."

Now a curved red arc appeared, skimming just above the asteroid belt, connecting the red dot of Mars to the green circle of the Jupiter station. "This is not your actual trajectory," Page pointed out. "Plotting the course will be up to you. Cadets, here is your mission: You are to fly the *Ishtar* from here to Voltaire Station, doing a category three survey of all asteroids within range of your sensors. You will have limited fuel and a deadline to meet. Your job will be to optimize the mission to retrieve the most information in the least time possible. Your departure time is 0800 tomorrow, so you will have approximately twenty-two hours to plan your mission. Details will be up to you. Questions?"

Roger had a question. Of course. "Sir, do we have to navigate that far from the Belt?"

"That is up to your discretion, Mr. Wells. However, I will point out that the *Ishtar* only has class-five shield capacity. If I were you, I'd rule out a direct run."

Roger sniffed.

Marta asked, "Captain Page, you said something about limited fuel. Why is that?"

"The assumption, Cadet Batanides, is that the *Ishtar* is a scout ship mapping an unfamiliar system. You've already done part of your survey and you are on the return leg to your mothership, represented by LaGrange Station Voltaire."

"Sir, how much fuel will we have?" Marta asked.

"You will find out at 0800 tomorrow," the captain said. Jean-Luc could not see his face, but he had the feeling that Page was smiling.

Jean-Luc's mind worked furiously. Not knowing the precise amount of fuel available meant that he would have to prepare more than one course trajectory. And—

"Sir," Cadet Captain Ran said, "I've heard that Nova crews occasionally run into surprises."

"Is that a question, Cadet Ran?"

"No, sir," the Kemoran said, her voice slow.

"Very well. I'll leave you to your planning. Terminate display. Room lights full." As the lights came up and the hologram faded, Captain Page's thin face materialized across the table from Jean-Luc. It wore a serious expression. "Let me say one last thing, cadets. You have worked hard, and I wish you well. But remember, Starfleet will not be riding herd on you. If you get yourselves into trouble, it will take several minutes to half an hour to get a craft to you. I don't like crews that get in trouble, and you would not like the kinds of ratings such a crew would receive. Watch yourselves and be prepared for anything. That is all."

An hour before launch, and on the cramped bridge of the *Ishtar,* Roger was all but yelling at Jean-Luc. "This is idiotic! You're going to sink us all. Picard, these courses are totally unacceptable!"

Jean-Luc's face was red with anger. "Mr. Wells, I have plotted a dozen different courses, allowing for as little as twenty-five percent fuel and for as much as eighty

80

percent. I'll fine-tune them as soon as our instruments are activated and—"

"You're taking us outside of the Belt!" Roger snarled. "We could just as easily penetrate the Belt and double the range of our survey!"

"We'll be within the fringes of the asteroid belt," Jean-Luc said, resisting the urge to yell. "If we took a more direct trajectory, we'd have to divert more power to the shields."

"He's a coward!" Roger said, turning to the other cadets as if for reinforcement. Marta looked away, embarrassed. Tom Franklin was scowling. Tabath Ran's alien expression was unreadable.

Jean-Luc turned to her. "Captain Ran, I will leave it up to you. Should I replot now, or would it be better to wait and get a precise reading when the ship powers up?"

The reptilian eyes flickered from Jean-Luc to Roger and back. Tabath licked her lips with a pointed black tongue. For a moment Jean-Luc thought she wasn't going to respond, but at last she said slowly, "Cadet Picard is correct, Number One. We will wait for ship power."

Roger threw his arms up in the air and turned his back on Jean-Luc. "All right! If I'm the only one who wants to get a decent grade on this—"

"Number One, I will want a full statement of mission and action plans for transmission as soon as possible. Please prepare to format such a document." Tabath Ran hesitated again, and then sank into the captain's seat.

With some muttering, Roger settled into the exec seat

beside her. He picked up a data padd and furiously began to program it, preparing a standard mission-statement template. Once they were actually under way, he would transmit the information back to Starfleet.

"Uh, I want to check the main tractor array power junction," Marta said. "Jean-Luc, will you help me?"

"Sure." Anything to get out of that cabin for a moment. And the thought that he would have to spend five or six hours cramped up with the others, and especially with Roger—Jean-Luc stopped worrying about it. He made sure that his science station was secure, then followed Marta down the narrow companionway. Halfway back to the small transporter array, she removed a deck plate and exposed a power junction.

He knelt beside it. "I'm not sure you can tell anything until we're off station power," he said.

"I didn't really want to check it," Marta whispered back. "That was just an excuse."

Jean-Luc took a deep breath. Cadets on training missions did not wear perfumes, but Marta had washed her hair in something that smelled rosy and pleasant. "Oh?" He allowed himself a crooked smile. "Roger is really being foolish, isn't he?"

Her dark eyes looked directly into his. "Roger? What are you talking about?"

He swallowed. "Uh—well, he was so unpleasant when he was arguing about my navigation. I assumed—"

"I'm concerned about Tabath, not about some silly macho competition between you and—"

"Macho competition? What are *you* talking about?"

Jean-Luc was stung. "He's the one acting like an idiot, not me."

Disgust flickered in those dark eyes. "Really? I'd call it a pretty close contest, myself." She bent over the power junction and plugged a Jeffries circuit tester in here and there. It verified only that the junction was capable of holding up under full power, plus a tolerance of fifty percent. They already knew that.

Jean-Luc took a deep breath. "What about Tabath?"

"If you're just going to argue—"

"No." He touched her shoulder, and she looked up. With a shock Jean-Luc saw that she had tears in her eyes. "You're really upset," he said. "Look, I'm sorry. What did you want to tell me?"

"Can't you tell there's something odd about her?"

With a frown Jean-Luc said, "Odd? I don't know. I've never had much to do with Kemorans, they're so standoffish."

"Well, I've been close to her for the last few days. We went over every plate and circuit of the *Ishtar*. She's sharp, Jean-Luc, and she's quick. Kemoran reaction time is fifty percent greater than human."

"So?"

Marta jerked her chin toward the cabin. "She's—she's slow. Something's wrong with her this morning. She's just not herself."

Jean-Luc grinned. "I doubt any of us are. She's just jumpy about doing well on the trip. Think about it; if this exercise means a lot to us first-year cadets, think how much more it must mean to a senior, and the captain of the ship at that. It's nerves, Marta."

Marta replaced the deck plate. Her doubtful expression showed that she was far from satisfied with Jean-Luc's explanation. At last, though, she sighed and muttered, "All right, if you say so. But let's remember what Captain Page said, Jean-Luc. We want to be very careful out there."

At precisely 0800:10, Marta reported from her engineering station: "*Ishtar* is under power, Captain."

"Thank you, Engineer." Tabath Ran activated the viewscreen. The control tower came into focus, with Captain Page standing in the foreground and half a dozen craft controllers visible behind him. "Cadet Captain Ran here, Docking Control. *Ishtar* ready for departure. We are waiting for clearance."

"Depart at your discretion, *Ishtar,*" Page responded. "Good luck out there."

The viewscreen shimmered, and they saw the rim of the station. Tabath paused for a second and then ordered, "Status report, Engineer."

Marta keyed a readout of the ship's status onto the viewscreen. Jean-Luc had a replica of it on his own computer readout. His eyes went straight to the fuel load. Fifty-three percent. Not bad—he might have wished for a little more, but even so, he would use or modify one of the trajectories he had already plotted.

"Release docking clamps," Tabath ordered.

"Clamps released," Marta reported.

After another momentary pause Tabath said, "Number One, take us out."

"Quarter reverse thrusters," Roger said at once. The *Ishtar*'s impulse engines throbbed to life, and the ship slowly backed out of dock, with a tense-looking Marta at the helm. Without turning, Roger said, "Navigation, give me a course for standard departure orbit."

Jean-Luc had anticipated the order, and he instantly returned with a bearing and mark.

"Helm, set course and engage thrusters at half," Roger said.

Jean-Luc shook his head. Although he knew they were in no danger of colliding with anything, half impulse was a fast speed for leaving dock, though not quite fast enough to call for a reprimand. Roger was testing the boundaries already.

Bradbury Station fell to one side in the screen, then the broad red face of Mars itself, craters and mountains and blue rippling rift sea, and then the stars were ahead of them. "Standard orbit," Tom Franklin reported.

"Good." Roger's voice took on an unpleasant edge: "Now, Mr. Picard, let's see your trajectory."

"I've plotted one for fifty percent fuel—"

The ship lurched, and Jean-Luc grabbed the console for support.

"What was that?" Tabath asked sharply.

"Fluctuation in the inertia damping system," Marta reported. "I'm on it."

Jean-Luc felt as if he were falling. He clenched his teeth to maintain control, but the sensation was exactly as if he were on an elevator that was moving down, faster and faster.

"Gravity's down to .80," Marta said, working hard at her console. "Now .75. We're losing five percent per seven seconds—"

"Fix it!" roared Roger. "If you foul this up—"

"Found a junction anomaly," Marta said. "I'm routing around it. Gravity is .62."

The lights flickered and Jean-Luc heard a whine of energy. Then the runaway turbolift began to slow. He felt his weight returning to normal.

"Captain," Tom Franklin said, "subspace communications are garbled. I can't establish contact with Bradbury Station."

Jean-Luc had also keyed in to the ship's computer as he pulled up his navigational trajectories. "Something here, too," he said to Tabath Ran. "The computer shows that our fuel consumption is running seven percent more than predicted."

For what seemed half a minute, Tabath Ran was quiet. Then she said, "Starfleet is testing us."

Roger turned toward Jean-Luc, a grin on his face. "Sure! I should have thought of that. These glitches are built in—we're supposed to solve them ourselves. Mr. Franklin, run communication diagnostics and belay your attempts to hail Bradbury Station until you've isolated the problem. Marta, make sure that our fuel consumption isn't really excessive. And Mr. Picard, lay in a course through the asteroid belt. We'll show them what we're made of!"

Sure we will, thought Jean-Luc. *Particularly if we hit an asteroid.*

Then what we're made of will be spread over a couple thousand cubic kilometers of dark, empty space.

CHAPTER

8

Their problems had only begun. Once the artificial gravity was back to normal, the fuel readings began to swing wildly. Subspace communications were still jammed, and the starboard sensor array was working at only half capacity. Tabath Ran gave increasingly sluggish suggestions, and Roger soon grew frantic.

"Let's take the problems one at a time," suggested Jean-Luc. "Now, the fuel sensors are routed through the starboard readout array. If Mr. Franklin can isolate the problem there, then we may find the false readings are just a part of the display malfunction."

Roger objected, "But he's on communications—"

"Which," interrupted Franklin, "aren't doing us any good at all. All subspace communication to Starfleet is down, though I can pick up routine traffic on commercial frequencies. I suggest we follow Mr. Picard's plan."

"I don't call it much of a plan," Roger muttered.

Marta said, "Well, if you have anything better—"

Roger threw his hands up in the air. "That's right, gang up on me. It's not *my* fault we're running into all this trouble."

"It is Starfleet," Tabath Ran murmured, her voice slow and sleepy. "I think we should do as Mr. Picard suggests."

"All right, fine," snapped Roger.

Marta asked, "What do you mean—'It's Starfleet'?"

Tabath replied, "They are testing us. They wish to make the exercise as difficult as possible. It is up to us to deal with all the problems." Her head swayed, as if she were dizzy.

"Are you all right?" Tom Franklin asked, his voice tight with concern.

Tabath closed her eyes. "Yes, we must deal with the— with the problems. However, I have another—problem— that is not their fault. Mr. Picard, give me a tricorder reading on myself, please."

Wondering what was up now, Jean-Luc took a tricorder from the instrument compartment and stood beside Tabath Ran to run the sensor scan. Since he knew almost nothing about Kemoran physiology, the resulting readout made little sense to him, but Tabath Ran took the device, looked at it, and sighed. "It is what I feared. I should have reported to sickbay three days ago, but I thought it was nothing, a minor virus. And I did not wish to miss this exercise."

"What's wrong?" Marta asked.

"A small ailment," Tabath told her. "Plate fever. A childhood dis—disease that lies latent in all my species. Most of us experience it during our first ten years of life. Unfortunately, I never had it until now. Perhaps the stress of the mission—" She yawned, showing her double row of sharp teeth. "I apologize to you. I must go dormant until the fever has passed—about twenty hours. Good luck. I—I cannot remain awake much longer." She activated the seat restraints. They would hold her secure, no matter what turbulence they encountered. She took several deep breaths, the iridescent sheen of blue and silver on her skin darkening as she did so.

"What!" Roger's voice was almost a screech. "You can't be serious!"

"You have the con, Mr. Wells," Tabath said without opening her eyes. "Sorry. I must rest. So—so sleepy . . ." Her voice trailed off.

"I've isolated the sensor readout problem," Tom Franklin announced. "It's in the subcontrol system routing, not in the sensors themselves, so we should be able to handle it. I'm initiating a repair sequence now."

"Navigator, what's our status?" snapped Roger.

Jean-Luc consulted his instruments. "I laid in course option four," he said. "As originally plotted, it would bring us in to Voltaire at 2023 hours. However, because we were delayed in going to full impulse, we are going to be late. To be exact, our present ETA is 2241 hours."

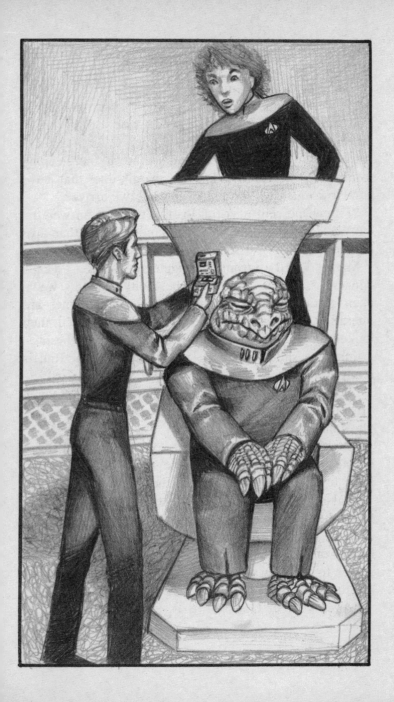

"More than two hours late?"

"If we stay on our original course," confirmed Jean-Luc. "It was plotted for our fuel load of fifty-three percent."

Roger sank into his seat and glared at the sleeping form of Tabath Ran. "What fuel margin does that leave us? How much will be left over when we arrive?"

"Fifteen percent of a full load." Jean-Luc answered.

"We'll cut it closer. We won't need more than five percent."

Marta looked up from her engineering station. "That's dangerous, Roger. And with the faulty readouts we've been getting, I can't guarantee that these engines are operating at full capacity. Besides—" She hesitated, then looked at Jean-Luc and said in a lower voice, "besides, I think we should go back to base. If Tabath Ran is really ill—"

"Forget that," said Roger. He glared at all of them. "It's another little Starfleet surprise. Don't you see that? She's in on it!"

Franklin paused in his work to look around and shake his head. "I don't think so. I've read about Kemoran plate fever, and she's shown all the symptoms."

"Faked!" growled Roger. "They're throwing everything they can at us. We've got to show we have what it takes. Mr. Picard, plot a new course through the fringes of the asteroid belt. Calculate trajectory with full power to the forward shields factored in. Mr. Franklin, are the sensors on line?"

"Aye, Number One."

With a fierce grin Roger said, "We'll show them. I want to arrive no later than our original ETA, and I want to deliver a full sensor scan to them."

Marta still looked troubled. "At least keep a medical scan on Tabath."

"I've already done so," Jean-Luc reported. "The tricorder shows she's in deep sleep, with a slightly elevated temperature and a depressed metabolism."

"Keep an eye on her, then," Roger said. "But I want to be on Voltaire Station no later than 2020 hours." He glowered at them all. "Consider that an order."

They coped. With one system after another showing a malfunction, an unconscious captain, and Roger's increasing irritability, the crew of the *Ishtar* still somehow coped. Five hours into the mission, they had almost everything under control. Tom Franklin still had been unable to establish communication with Starfleet, although all of his systems checked out correctly on diagnostics. It was clear that Starfleet simply did not choose to talk with them—and Roger absolutely forbade Franklin to send any hint of a distress signal, any mention of Tabath's illness.

The tricorder readings showed that she was in no real danger, just sound asleep. For nearly half an hour Jean-Luc hoped they had overcome all the serious difficulties. And then, as they burrowed their way through the outer edge of the asteroid belt, something else happened. Franklin, still working over the communications system, looked up sharply. "Number One, we're receiving a distress call."

"What? Where's the point of origin?"

Franklin checked his instruments. "Deep inside the Belt."

"Here?" Roger asked, his voice raspy with exasperation. "Impossible. What ship would be in the middle of the Belt?"

"It's coming from an asteroid mining scout ship," Franklin said, and he gave the distressed ship's mark and bearing.

Jean-Luc turned from his console. "That's only a few minutes away, deeper in the Belt. It's possible something's wrong there."

With a disgruntled shrug Roger snapped, "Put it on screen."

The viewscreen, which had been displaying a starfield crossed by tumbling asteroids, shimmered into a static-streaked picture of a haggard man. "—calling any vessel within range," he was saying. "We need immediate assistance."

"Starfleet training ship *Ishtar* here," Roger said. "Cadet Roger Wells commanding. What is your trouble?"

"Thank God!" the man said. "I'm Gene Sayre, assistant mineralogist with the Worrell Mining Commission. My pilot and I are stuck in close orbit around a nickel-iron asteroid—we've had a thruster malfunction, and it will take most of a day to repair. Trouble is, we don't have that kind of time. We've detected a gravitational anomaly coming our way from system north, and we need immediate evacuation."

Roger turned to Jean-Luc. "Science officer, can you confirm the anomaly?"

Jean-Luc adjusted the long-range sensors. He blinked at the incredible readings. "Confirmed," he said. "Something very small with great mass is coming our way at—at point seven light speed!"

"Put that on screen, full magnification."

They all stared at the screen. Nothing. The starfield, black space, and nothing.

Or—was that a strange ripple effect? When viewed

from outside the atmosphere of a planet, stars do not twinkle, but something made one small group of stars seem to shimmer and dance. "There," Franklin said, adjusting the screen to put the odd effect in the center. "Gravity waves strong enough to bend light. Something's coming, all right, and faster than anything I've ever seen. I'm confirming—yes, my reading agrees with Mr. Picard's. The object is moving at more than point seven."

They all looked at him. Practically nothing in nature moved at three-quarters of the speed of light—nothing except starships, certain subatomic particles, and—

"A black comet!" Tom Franklin said.

"Don't be ridiculous. There's never been a report of one in this spiral arm," snapped Roger.

"Ishtar," repeated Sayre plaintively, and Franklin brought his stressed image back onto the screen. "Our instruments show that the anomaly will pass within a thousand kilometers of us in fifteen minutes. We need your help immediately."

"Audio off," Roger growled. Franklin complied.

"I don't understand," Marta said. "What's a black comet?"

Jean-Luc glanced at her. She was pale with tension. "A black comet is sometimes called a neutron core," he explained. "They're very rare. Starfleet has confirmed only two, both in the Beta Quadrant. Those were very small, only a few meters across, but extraordinarily dense, with gravitational fields at least as great as the sun's. And they move in enormous orbits around Galactic Center, but inclined to the Galactic plane."

"I thought you were the science officer, not the science teacher," Roger said, his voice dripping sarcasm.

"Oh, be quiet, Roger," Franklin said. "Some scientists thought they were small pieces of broken-up neutron stars, but now most people believe they're leftover dense matter from the Big Bang. Anyway, they've got unbelievable gravitational fields. They suck normal matter right into themselves, like black holes."

"A thousand kilometers won't be enough, will it?" Jean-Luc asked.

Shaking his head, Franklin replied, "At a thousand kilometers, something with that much mass will rip the asteroid to pieces—and the ship. We've got to divert."

Jean-Luc nodded. "I agree. We have only twelve and a half minutes. If we alter course now, we can barely make it and escape with the two miners. It will take all our power."

"What do you mean—all our power?" demanded Roger. His face was flushed, his fists balled.

"We won't have sufficient fuel to make the Voltaire rendezvous," Jean-Luc explained. "We'll have just enough for life support for three days. But Starfleet will come looking for us—"

"No!" Roger pounded the arm of his seat. "No. It's just a test. There's no anomaly—they've rigged our sensors to give us a false reading. We'll maintain course."

Marta said, "Roger, I agree with Jean-Luc. What if it's not a test? If we fail to respond to a real distress call, we're washed up as far as Starfleet goes. We couldn't even get jobs as merchant spacers!"

Roger snarled. "All right, all right. Let them call Starfleet and—"

"No time," Franklin said. "By the time a Starfleet vessel could penetrate the Belt this far, it wouldn't matter. They'd be dead. And anyway, the gravity waves are interfering with subspace communications. I doubt that Starfleet could even hear them."

"Then—then divert," Roger said. "No, wait—maintain course, but—or we could—" He looked at the others, doubt and fear in his eyes. "You know what they're doing to us, with all these emergencies. It's the *Kobayashi Maru* all over again!"

Jean-Luc felt a moment of doubt. Every Academy cadet knew of the legendary *Kobayashi Maru* scenario, a training exercise in which nothing a cadet did could succeed. Could it be? Possibly. But if it wasn't—

"We have only ten minutes left," Jean-Luc said.

"Do something, Jean-Luc," Marta said. "Give the word, and I'll change course—"

"Shut up!" Roger shouted. "That's mutiny!"

Jean-Luc looked at him. Roger was sweating, his eyes darting frantically. Roger was right: For Jean-Luc to assume command, or even the upperclassman Tom Franklin, they all would have to mutiny against Roger's authority, breaking one of the oldest laws of the service. If this were just a test, that was a step that could well mean the end of their Starfleet dreams.

But against that stood two lives in danger.

What to do? Jean-Luc had no time to think, but he had to make a decision.

What to do?

CHAPTER

9

"Permission to make a suggestion?" Jean-Luc asked.

Roger, face glistening with sweat, fair hair plastered to his forehead, stared at him as if he had made a physical threat. For a moment Jean-Luc thought Roger was going to scream at him, or perhaps even strike out. Then he made a visible effort to gain control over himself. "Granted," he said, his tone anything but friendly.

Jean-Luc rose and went to Roger's side. He bent over and whispered as Franklin and Marta looked on. He could tell they were puzzled, maybe even a little hurt by his secretiveness, but his only hope of pulling this off lay with making Roger at least appear to be the decision-maker. After a few seconds Roger nodded, and Jean-Luc went back to his science station. Roger cleared his throat and said, "Engineering, Navigation will give you a new course. Lay it in. Power up all tractor beams, and make sure forward shields are at full strength."

Before a bewildered-looking Marta could respond, Jean-Luc sent her the new coordinates. Marta adjusted the helm, and the *Ishtar* immediately changed direction, streaking deeper into the Belt. "Full power to forward shields," Roger ordered.

"Aye, sir," Marta responded. "Shields at full power and holding."

Jean-Luc had altered the sensor scan, making the *Ishtar* viewscreen look back in the direction from which they had come. "The anomaly is approaching quite fast," he said. "This is going to be awfully close—I'll need Mr. Franklin's help to coordinate the tractor beams."

"Make it so."

"I'm glad to help. Only, what are we doing?" Franklin asked.

Jean-Luc grinned fiercely. "I hope we're going for a ride. In a few seconds the black comet is going to come streaking in off to port, and it will pass by at the extreme limit of tractor range. We have to lock on to it with a tractor beam as soon as it's in striking distance, and hold on to it after it passes."

"Are you serious? We can't drag anything close to that mass. We can't even make it swerve a single centimeter!" Franklin objected.

"No, but Mr. Wells thinks it can drag *us*. Its gravity will pull us down into the Belt, without our using any power. In five minutes we'll power up and go into a tight slingshot orbit around the anomaly. We'll get to the miners' ship roughly twenty seconds before the comet does—so we'll have only one chance to beam those two aboard. Our trajectory will fling us back out above the plane of the Belt. Then, at three-quarters cruising speed, we should have enough fuel left to make it to Voltaire Station—barely."

"Full power available on all tractor beams," reported Marta. "Shields are holding. We're hitting random debris from the Belt."

Franklin bent tensely over his controls. "Waiting for the target," he said.

Jean-Luc glanced at Roger Wells, who looked forlorn and frightened. "Sir, perhaps you had better tell Mr. Sayre and his pilot to stand by. We should rendezvous with them in"—Jean-Luc checked a chronometer read-out—"six minutes and seventeen seconds."

"Open communi—" began Roger. Then he grinned, though it was a sickly, green-around-the-gills grin. "Belay that order. You're busy. I'll take care of it." From his auxiliary control panel Roger called up Sayre's image again and explained matters to him. The picture was barely readable, and the sound crackled and sputtered. Communications were terrible because the approaching anomaly was disturbing the normal lines of space-time, but after Roger had repeated his message several times, Sayre understood and said they would both stand by, with their locator broadcasting signals at full power. Roger signed off.

"Here it comes," Franklin announced. "Engaging tractor—missed!"

"Try again!" shouted Wells.

"Aye-aye. Got it! Hang on—this is going to mess up our inertial damping system."

For an agonizingly long half a minute, nothing changed. They all waited, tense and silent.

Then Jean-Luc felt a strange sensation at the pit of his stomach. Ordinarily, when a ship had its inertial damping field on, the passengers could feel no acceleration. A ship being pummeled by energy might have enough field fluctuation to toss its crew around, but under ordinary conditions, everything was rock solid.

Now, though, it was like being on the highest hill of the biggest roller-coaster in the universe. One had the sensation of a pause, then an endless forward drop, going faster and faster. Jean-Luc found himself gasping for breath.

The viewscreen showed the stars blurring as the *Ishtar* vibrated from the strain of holding on to the black comet. The anomaly itself was still invisible, but Jean-Luc was probing it with all sensors.

What he read was incredible. The entire mass had no more volume than a small shuttlecraft, barely more than the *Ishtar*. But it was so dense that it was as if the entire Earth, and another dozen planets like it, had been crushed down to that size. Anything on the surface of that tiny body would be smashed by gravity.

A human being would be reduced to a one-molecule thick film of bone, flesh, and blood, all pulverized and spread over the unimaginable surface.

"Look at that!" Marta cried.

Jean-Luc stared at the viewscreen, now looking forward again. A tumbling asteroid dissolved, pulled into a dusty stream of matter, friction heating it to incandescent brightness, as the black comet pulled it in. Even its dying glare could not illuminate the small mass at the heart of the disturbance. Jean-Luc tore his fascinated gaze away and looked at his readouts. The doomed asteroid had been just within a thousand kilometers of the comet. Its fate would be the same as that of the two miners if the *Ishtar*'s desperate attempt failed.

"If this is a holographic simulation," Franklin grumbled, "I think I'll ask for planet-side service."

They wouldn't do that to us, Jean-Luc thought. Or would they? The *Kobayashi Maru* scenario had certainly washed out its share of would-be Starfleet officers, and that was all simulation.

"What's our speed?" Roger asked.

Marta instantly answered, "We're at point seven light speed—going faster than safety margins for a Nova-class trainer. Shields are holding, though."

They *had* to hold.

By now Jean-Luc could detect innumerable impacts against the energy shields, fragments of the destroyed asteroid, pebble-sized pieces of matter that could zip through duranium like a knife through butter at the speed they were traveling. A hull breach could be dealt with on a starship, but on a trainer it would mean instant, nasty death for everyone inside.

"We're coming up on the time to begin our burn,"

Jean-Luc said. "Should we prepare to beam the two miners aboard?"

"Yes," Roger said. "Make it so."

Make it so. That old, Earth-bound command beloved in the British navy. Despite their danger, despite their frantic hurry, Jean-Luc could not help smiling a little. He liked the sound of that old-fashioned order.

"I'll go to the transporter station and operate it from there," Franklin said. "Better chance of a clear lock from the primary controls."

He squeezed into the corridor, and a moment later his voice came over the shipboard communication system: "Transporters ready. If we can get within range, we should be able to grab them. I'm picking up both of their signals, loud and clear."

"Transport them as soon as we're close enough," Jean-Luc said. "You won't have more than four or five seconds."

"Understood."

Jean-Luc kept a steady eye on his navigation readouts. The computer helped—he couldn't have done anything without it—but it finally came down to one vital decision: his.

A miscalculation of just a fraction of one second could be the difference between life and death.

Jean-Luc's muscles tensed. His heart pounded loud in his ears. "Prepare to engage engines, full thrust, current heading," he said. "Ready on my mark: Five. Four. Three. Two. One. Engage!"

The *Ishtar*'s engines surged to full power.

"Cut tractor beams!" Jean-Luc yelled. Marta dropped them at once.

The little ship was now free of its unseen companion. Balancing acceleration and centripetal force against gravity, it swirled around in an orbit that carried it faster and faster, hurtling toward the far side of the black comet. And toward the stranded miners, who by now must be terrified, seeing the chaos the incoming mass was making among the asteroids.

Roger was still monitoring communications. "We're coming," he said. "Stand by. We'll energize as soon as we're within range."

No response. Perhaps the miners had not even received Roger's message. It was impossible to tell.

The viewscreen had dissolved into gray and black streaks of static, its systems strained past their tolerance points by the gravitational waves put out by the black comet. Jean-Luc could hear the creak and groan of metal, the complaint of a ship far exceeding its design standards.

The ship communicator chirped, and Franklin's voice said, "Locked on to two targets, energizing."

"We're around the comet!" yelled Marta. "Speed is point eight light and holding!"

Jean-Luc watched the display of his navigational computer. The comet, marked by an ugly red spiral of gravity, had never been closer than now. The tidal forces of its gravity made the *Ishtar* scream in protest. The whole ship hummed with tension.

Like a Valusian skitter-mouse fleeing from a charging

cobra-cat, the *Ishtar* flashed right in front of the comet's wave of destruction, then arced back up and away from it. Jean-Luc checked his calculations, double-checked them. "We're free of the gravitational field," he said, relief in his voice. "Heading out of the asteroid belt."

"Slowing to cruising speed," Marta reported. "We're showing lots of minor damage. Nothing serious enough to threaten the ship, though."

With a sigh Jean-Luc read out their new position. "We're far off our original course."

For a moment everyone on the bridge was silent.

"Did we get them?" Marta asked, sounding strained and upset.

Franklin answered right away: "Affirmative. I'm opening the hatch to the crew quarters so that Mr. Sayre and Mr. Wilmot can rest and have some food. They're worn out."

Sayre's voice came through over Franklin's communicator: "Captain? Thank you. For a few minutes there, we thought we were dead ducks."

"You're welcome," said Roger, with a glance at Jean-Luc.

"You put on one whale of a show of piloting," Sayre said.

With a pale smile Roger said, "Thank my crew. They're the ones who made it work."

A few moments later Tom Franklin returned and slipped into his seat. "They're exhausted," he said. "Both of them had been suited up, outside their ship, working on the thrusters, for eighteen hours."

"Why didn't they call for help earlier?" asked Marta.

Franklin shrugged as he began to run his hands over the communication control panel. "You know miners. The last of the great individualists. Anyway, they thought they could repair their ship. Probably could have, too, without the interference of our heavy visitor. Well, they can rest now." He shook his head. "Wouldn't you know? Now Starfleet is signaling us, but our transmission system is really down."

"Can you repair it?" asked Roger.

"I'll see what I can do. But we took quite a shaking during that pass. I'm betting we'll have to hold off on our explanations until after we dock."

"Speaking of that," said Roger, "what's our course going to be?"

Jean-Luc had been working out their fuel reserves. He gave a mark and bearing. "That will put us into Voltaire four hours late," he said. "But it's the only way we can get there without having to drift in."

"Get us to Voltaire in one piece," Roger said, his voice drained and empty. "That's all I ask."

"We will be four hours late," Jean-Luc repeated.

"As long as we get there under our own power, I don't care. It's not going to be much of a celebration for me, anyway," said Roger, and he fell into a brooding silence.

He looked like someone who had just read his own death sentence.

CHAPTER

10

"I don't deserve this," Tabath Ran said, squirming uncomfortably.

"If Starfleet says you deserve it, then you do," Tom Franklin responded. "Just relax and accept it."

Jean-Luc paced back and forth, wondering where in the world Marta was. He, Tom, and Tabath were in a small room backstage at Scobee Hall. In a few minutes they would have to go out onstage and—well, that would take care of itself. Right now, he had other things to worry about.

He ran back over the incredible events of the past six days. The *Ishtar* had limped into Voltaire Station under its own power, but just barely. Captain Page waited for them at the docking station. "So here you are," he said as the crew stumbled out—or at least the conscious members of it, because Tabath was still asleep at that point. "I'll expect a full explanation."

Explanations there were in plenty. As it developed, Starfleet could have sent a fast vessel to pick them all up not long after they emerged from the asteroid belt. "Only," Captain Page explained with just the hint of a twinkle in his eye, "I expected you would want to bring your ship back, or what's left of it, at any rate."

Both of the miners were well, and within two days, so was Tabath, except for a lingering embarrassment at being laid up by a childhood disease at the most crucial part of their trip. By the time they boarded a Starfleet shuttle for the trip back to Earth, they had already learned that a starship had been dispatched to follow the black comet. As soon as it was a comfortable distance from the solar system, the ship would attempt to destroy it with antimatter torpedoes.

On the trip back to Earth—a much more comfortable trip on a real Starfleet vessel than on a trainer—Captain Page told them that they had done well. "You probably noticed that we like to throw cadet crews certain little problems on these training missions," he said, not smiling. "Well, we didn't anticipate that one would come roaring in from interstellar space. You succeeded in dealing with it, and you brought your ship back. I don't think any of the other crews will have performance ratings quite as high as yours."

And none did.

Now they were to receive commendation ribbons, and two of the crew—Marta and Roger—were late.

Jean-Luc stopped his pacing and opened the hall door. There she was! He went out to meet her. "Where have you been?" he demanded. "They'll call us out any minute now—"

"It's Roger," Marta said simply.

Jean-Luc looked down at his feet. He puffed out his cheeks and straightened his tunic. "Where is he?"

Roger was outside, sitting on a bench beneath one of Boothby's beloved California yews. The cadet sat slumped over, his face mottled and his eyes red. Jean-Luc came over and sat next to him. Roger didn't look up. "Go away," he said, very distinctly.

"The ceremony is due to begin," Jean-Luc said.

"So go. It won't matter to me."

"What do you mean?"

Roger glared at him. "It means you've won, all right? I'm resigning from the Academy. I hope you're happy."

Jean-Luc leaned back and looked up at the deep blue sky. "We were never in competition," he said.

"Ha!" Roger wiped his eyes. "Everyone said I had it easy because my father is a government minister. Well, I studied! And I was the best—the best! But then you came along, and you did things so much easier than I did—"

Jean-Luc laughed.

Roger stared at him, deep misery in his eyes. "Don't make fun of me!"

In a soft voice Jean-Luc said, "I'm not. The joke is

that I thought that very same thing about you. You never
seemed to have to struggle, and I'm—well, I'm a bit of
a plodder. Sometimes."

A puzzled look came into Roger's eyes. "You mean
you thought that I was that smart?"

Jean-Luc nodded.

Roger laughed—a harsh, bitter laugh, but a laugh still.
"And all this time I was knocking myself out to keep
that tiny edge over you!"

Jean-Luc stood in the cool shade of the fir. "Perhaps

the secret is in working together, not against each other. That's how we did it on the *Ishtar*."

"How you saved my neck, you mean, when I froze."

"No. How we all worked together—*together,* Roger—and saved those two miners, and the ship, and one another. That's what Starfleet is all about. Come on. You're not going to quit. You're too good for that."

Roger got to his feet, but he still looked stubborn. "Tell me this: How did you figure all that out about the comet? I was scared out of my wits."

"So was I," confessed Jean-Luc. "But you still have to do something, even when you're scared. I tried to follow Mr. Spock's advice. Remember?"

Light dawned in Roger's eyes. "You made an ally of an enemy by letting the comet tow us to the miners. You made a crisis into an opportunity by rescuing them and the ship."

"And I learned from the experience," Jean-Luc said. "Now I know what being part of a team—part of a Starfleet crew—means. I think you should learn the same lesson."

"Guys!" It was Marta, frantically gesturing. "They're calling us!"

Jean-Luc stared at Roger. "Well?"

Roger mustered a grin, a ghost of his old jaunty one. "Well—race you to the door!"

After the ceremony Jean-Luc wandered off alone. It was all very nice, standing onstage, having your classmates clap for you, but he needed time to absorb it, to adjust. He strolled aimlessly for a quarter of an hour. He wound up at the triangular bed where he had helped Boothby with the rose sets. They seemed to have taken hold. Of course, none were in bloom. They looked like dry bundles of thorny sticks, to tell the truth. But all were green, all alive.

Jean-Luc felt a hand on his shoulder. "You plant well," said Boothby.

"Thank you."

"And I heard about the little celebration back in Scobee Hall, too. I suppose I should congratulate you. Of course, starship captains are a dime a dozen, you understand. Good gardeners are rare."

Jean-Luc looked at the old man. "What does that mean—'a dime a dozen'?"

Boothby sniffed. "Means there's more than enough of you young smartypants for the whole galaxy and then some. Well, congratulations on finding the right soil at last. I hope something good grows in it."

Jean-Luc frowned. "Soil? For the roses, you mean?"

"For yourself," Boothby returned. "Are you sure you're really as smart as they say?"

Jean-Luc shook his head. "No. I've never been sure of that."

"Good. Maybe that will keep you humble." Boothby cleared his throat. "Think of a Starfleet commander as a kind of rare plant. He's got to find the right soil to grow in. Yours seems to be wherever leadership is needed. Is that clear enough?"

"Clear enough."

"Then get out of here. Your friends are waiting at your dormitory to throw you a surprise party."

Jean-Luc stared at the old man. "How did you know that?"

"I know everything!" Boothby snapped. "I'm a gardener!"

Jean-Luc went on his way. He turned once to wave, but Boothby was on his knees, head bent low, his skillful hands on a struggling plant, helping it grow stronger, healthier, and straighter.

Feeling strong and healthy himself, Jean-Luc ran the rest of the way to his surprise party.

About the Authors

BRAD and BARBARA STRICKLAND are a husband-and-wife writing team from Oakwood, Georgia. Brad has written or co-written eighteen novels and more than sixty short stories, including two *Star Trek: Deep Space Nine* novels for young readers, *The Star Ghost* and *Stowaways*. Barbara makes her writing debut as co-author of the two *Starfleet Academy* novels *Starfall* and *Nova Command*.

Both Stricklands are teachers. Brad is an Associate Professor of English at Gainesville College, and Barbara teaches second grade at Myers Elementary School. They have a son, Jonathan; a daughter, Amy; and numerous pets. In addition to writing, Brad likes travel, sailing, and photography, and Barbara is a great *Star Trek* fan and enjoys crafts. She won first prize for children's costumes at the World Science Fiction Convention in Atlanta, Georgia. Both husband and wife know how to bathe a ferret.

About the Illustrator

TODD CAMERON HAMILTON is a self-taught artist who has resided all his life in Chicago, Illinois. He has been a professional illustrator for the past ten years, specializing in fantasy, science fiction, and horror. Todd is the current president of the Association of Science Fiction and Fantasy Artists. His original works grace many private and corporate collections. He has co-authored two novels and several short stories. When he is not drawing, painting, or writing, his interests include metalsmithing, puppetry, and teaching.